TALES OF HARPER

Best Wishes
Malcolm L. Wilkinson

Tales of Harper

A collection of Short Stories and Poems

Malcolm L. Wilkinson

Copyright © 2014 by Malcolm L. Wilkinson.

Cover photo by Jane W. Wilkinson

Library of Congress Control Number:		2014904894
ISBN:	Hardcover	978-1-4931-8584-9
	Softcover	978-1-4931-8585-6
	eBook	978-1-4931-8583-2

All rights reserved. No part of this book may be reproduced or transmitted in any form or by any means, electronic or mechanical, including photocopying, recording, or by any information storage and retrieval system, without permission in writing from the copyright owner.

This is a work of fiction. Names, characters, places and incidents either are the product of the author's imagination or are used fictitiously, and any resemblance to any actual persons, living or dead, events, or locales is entirely coincidental.

This book was printed in the United States of America.

Rev. date: 03/20/2014

To order additional copies of this book, contact:
Xlibris LLC
1-888-795-4274
www.Xlibris.com
Orders@Xlibris.com

Contents

The Importance of Story 9
How Grandpa Wheeler Came to Stay in Harper (1910) 10
One Summer Evening in 1944 12
Legion 1949 13
The Other Side of Legend 18
How I Came to Leave Harper 1952 19
Walking Home From The Harper Theatre (1954) 24
His Minnie 29
The Railroad Watch 1955 30
Broken Crutches (1956) 37
Who Says Dreams Can't Come True 1979 40
Comeuppance 1985 46
Forgetting Misty 1989 53
Harper Lake 55
Kichwa Kubwa 1992 56
The Call of Old Ways 1995 60
Love in City 67
Dealing with Slight Hope 1999 69
Lures 2002 75
May Margaret's Christmas Extravaganza 2009 81
Another Christmas Extravaganza 2010 89
The Small and Shrinking World of Barney Blaine 2010 95
That Moment 100

Dedication

The poems and stories in this book are dedicated to my grandparents Amile and Ida, William Caston and Anne Elizabeth; my parents Morris and Ontie ; and to all my aunts and uncles: George Bonnie and Audrey, Maggie and Marley, Claude and Mattie, Hoyt and Annie May, Jennie Lee, Gladys and Truly, Hilary and Frances, Ray and Marguerite, Juanita and Jimmy, Randolph and Violet, Ora Lee and Tex. While all of this work is fictional I must admit their lives and the stories they told directly influenced my imagination.

The author expresses his gratitude to Sarah Shope for her instruction and encouragement and to the members of her creative writing classes who offered support and critique over the years. I must give a special thanks to Karen Swim for helping with the formatting and review of this work. and to my daughter, Jane Wilkinson, whose beautiful cover art and assistance in publication made this book possible.

The Importance of Story

My father never spoke of his father.

The few things I learned about my grandfather
came from little things my mother said.
Once during an argument she told my dad,
"You're just like Old Hank, you're probably keeping
a woman up in Tottertown too."
When I asked my dad about this he had nothing to say.

I have seen pictures of grandfather and he looks like a kind man.
But he left his family and moved to another state with a woman named Parmee.
She inherited his money and left it to her brother.

That's all I know about grandfather.

You, my son, should know more of your grandfather.

So sit back and listen.
Take off your shoes if you want.
I guarantee you will be glad we talked.
Maybe not today, but one day when you have children
and you tell them the story of me.

How Grandpa Wheeler Came to Stay in Harper (1910)

The urge to break free came during summer vacation after he had completed the eighth grade. Each night he found it harder to come in from the fields surrounding his house, often lying on his back fully awake, learning from the various skies. As September approached he sensed a destiny that lay beyond the confines of home. The night before the first day of the new school year he labored over a farewell letter, finally giving up on explanations and settling for a two-word promise, "I'll write."

From the beginning he used the rails, hopping trains with unknown destinations, always glad to arrive where they took him. He spent countless nights in hobo camps sleeping under whatever sky nature offered, often cold and hungry, but always thankful for the freedom he had chosen. Many mornings he awoke confused and bewildered by his solitude, longing for old friends or family, only to shrug it off while gathering his things for a quick departure.

Around campfires late into the night, the men shared tales of big cities and open spaces, of strangers who had befriended them and family members left behind, of lonely nights and rip-roaring adventures. Their stories accompanied by cricket songs took on the measure of poetry and sent him to sleep having sufficiently dreamed for the night.

During his sixth year out, for some reason, perhaps to see first hand the places he had heard about, he began to plan his travels. Discipline crept into his life. At first he resisted and gave up on some plans so he could stay longer with certain comrades, but gradually he fell into a pattern of scheduling his time and setting priorities. Somewhere in this transformation he took a real job; not working a few hours a day for a meal or a piece of clothing, but duty with set hours and responsibilities. He promised himself he would stay only until he made enough to finance his next adventure.

Six months later, he remained in the employment of the Illinois Central Railroad, loading baggage on and off passenger trains. In a town named Harper, located almost halfway between Jackson, Mississippi and New Orleans, he took up citizenship. He met a girl. In her he felt some of the same fascination he had experienced on the road. One night, being particularly vulnerable to the effect of the stars, he told her he loved her and could not live without her and wanted to spend the rest of his life with her. Perhaps she saw no better opportunity so she married him.

They lived with her parents, a situation which prompted him to solicit the help of a fellow baggage-loader who was skilled in carpentry. Together, each evening after work, the two constructed a three-room house. Within a year he and his wife moved into their new home, and over the next few years, she gave birth to three children.

At first, his responsibility as a father kept his mind off the road. But when the youngest child finished high school, the urge to move on grew stronger. He fought it, telling himself he really did love her.

One night they were sitting in the front porch swing, his arm around her shoulder, talking about nothing in particular. As the moon forced its way past a low, thick cloud, bringing a dim color to the world around them, she reached for his hand and took it to her lap. They sat motionless in the swing, neither speaking.

After a while, she stood and turned, gazing into his eyes. He had not spoken his feeling for her in many years, but tonight his look and touch seemed to give her a renewed confidence. As was their habit, she went to bed, leaving him to his adoration of the night.

In the morning, when she realized he had not come to bed, she hurried barefoot and robeless into the kitchen. She found him seated at the table, staring ahead, unaware of her arrival. As she walked toward him, he turned to her and he smiled.

Later that day while tending to some brush that needed burning, he took from his pockets several wads of paper, failed attempts to justify his yearning, and added them to the fire, sending their message on the journey he could not take.

One Summer Evening in 1944

The old man took his place
in the adirondack chair down by
the victory garden and looked up
at the house where he had lived his life.
In the kitchen window his wife,
pink in the light of a hanging 40 watt bulb,
stood at the sink peeling potatoes for his dinner.
Surrounded by the sounds of early evening
he thought of love and how it had come back
to the simplicity of his childhood.

The old woman stood in the kitchen
making dinner for her husband.
She could see him in his usual place,
down by the victory garden.
A recent frailty seemed to have taken him over.
He seemed smaller, dimmer in approaching dark.
A little shiver ran her spine.
And for the first time came
acceptance of Fate, hers and his.
For the first time she forgave.

LEGION
1949

And Jesus asked him, saying, "What is thy name?" And he said, "Legion": because many devils were entered into him.

They came for Uncle Legion on a mild December day in 1947; three men in a dark green sedan with license plates issued by the state of Louisiana to a car purchased for transporting crazy people to the asylum. Please do not bristle at my term for describing my uncle's illness for this was a common description for any ailment with behavior not conforming to that expected from a normal citizen of the community. Many people were never called for by the state employees nor moved away from the normals. Uncle Legion was not so lucky.

The next year on the first of June, Uncle Legion's birthday, we (his mother, father, and I) came to visit him. He was thirty-six years old. Though I had not reached my twelfth year on earth, it had been much on my mind—this thing about Legion's confinement—for I remember him when his actions were not to be questioned.

John Legion Campbell was born into a happy home, blessed with a loving mother and a father hell bent on providing for his wife and children, often working extra hours or extra jobs to overcome his inability to enter into a profession, which would automatically insure wealth. His lack of advanced education had seen to that. They called him Legion; his father was called John, to avoid confusion in the community. Grandmother Campbell issued a warning. The name Legion was in her mind associated with demons and she would not call him that. She was the one who cautioned them about making faces that could be frozen by some cosmic frost into a permanent disfiguration. They were not to sit in wheelchairs or walk with a limp or in any way mimic a disease or infirmity of any nature. So no one really took her seriously about the name.

Legion grew straight and tall and by high school, his speed and strength enabled him to participate in team sports. His strong throwing ability made him first choice for quarterback in the fall and pitcher in the spring. The citizens of Harper agreed he was the All-American boy. A scholarship to the state university was offered to him and he accepted. I heard little of his college days for these were times Legion did not share with family. They were surely his own years not to be distributed to the scrutiny of others.

When Legion came back to Harper from the university, he brought with him a bride. He called her Lila and introduced her as my wife, Delilah. She was all glitter and flamboyance, what seemed to be a bright star in the dark skies of Harper life. They seemed happy, at least for the first year. About six months after they returned to our town, Uncle Legion rushed Aunt Lila to the hospital in the next county and there she presented him with a baby girl. They called her Margie. Everyone said she was the prettiest baby ever born in the state of Mississippi. Another little girl, they named her Deborah, came a little over a year later. When she was just a year old the war came from out of nowhere.

It was December the seventh, 1941, and we were sitting in the living room of grandfather's house listening to a New York concert on his Philco radio. You know what happened: the announcement of an attack on Pearl Harbor. We were suddenly at war. This is not to say there weren't warning signs, but the finality of the commentator's words came as unexpected as a tornado when all we had looked for was dark clouds and perhaps a stiff breeze.

Within a few months Legion joined several young men from Harper as they were called to duty. A star was placed in the front window of grandfather's house. When we heard from Uncle Legion it was clear he was somewhere in Europe; the details were cloaked in secrecy. Aunt Lila cried when he left, but within a year she was bouncing around the few nightspots Harper had to offer. This was a circumstance which could not be confined from the attention of the citizens of Harper. Word soon came to Grandmother Campbell. Her approach to Aunt Lila held no delay, her words were not softened to prevent insult or hurt. Lila, in what appeared to be retaliation to her mother-in-law's harshness, revealed her pregnancy. Grandmother did not need her fingers to count the months Uncle Legion had been gone.

"Who is the father?" Grandmother spoke the word father with all the vehemence she could summon to her Christian tongue.

"It's no matter. I'm leaving this crumby town."

"What about your children?"

"They're only half mine. I'll leave them until Legion gets home. Then we'll work it out."

"And who are you going to leave them with?"

"With my husband's parents. How can I take care of them? I have been run out of town with no means of support."

"You have run yourself out of town. And I think you have shown you have discovered a means of support. God help you and God help our son."

Lila bristled. "Your son is no angel. You must know he married me out of duress. We were not married until he realized I was expecting."

Grandmother took the two girls and cared for them until the war was over. Uncle Legion returned a different man than we had seen off in 1942. He accepted the news of his wife's infidelity and quick departure with unexpected calmness. It was as if he was not surprised at his wife's behavior. A man who did not go to battle had taken his management position at the garment factory. Legion accepted a lesser position and set about fulfilling the responsibility of fatherhood. For a few months things appeared to go well.

It was at church one Sunday his true condition came out for all to see. During the first hymn he began to tear up. And by the reading of the Bible verses his crying was uncontrolled and the people sitting around him began to show their discomfort by squirming in their seats and whispering to their neighbors. Grandfather, who sang bass in the choir, stood and walked around to the steps and down to the congregation. He took Uncle Legion by the arm and led him out of the church.

Not a month later the dark green sedan arrived and my uncle was carried away to the best care available at the time.

At the Shady Rest Home for the Insane a hefty woman in a plain black dress I took to be a uniform led us into a large room. The room had at least a dozen windows all looking out on the green forest that surrounded the facility. Patients in various dress sat on wooden benches, most stared straight ahead. A chorus of coughs and throat clearing filled the chamber. One woman, rail thin and frumpily dressed, practiced the scales. Do—re-mi mi mi mi mi—fa sol—la—ti—do. She seemed to get stuck on the mi. It occurred to me this was something I had seen in a movie, a scene with an opera singer warming up.

Uncle Legion was smiling. There could be no conflict in his life—it would've shown in some way, be it subtle or profound—for he sat there as happy as a ten year old. He was aware that it was his birthday because he told us how glad he was we remembered. I could not help wondering what was going on in his mind.

The next time we visited Uncle Legion, a few months later, there were obvious changes in his appearance and mannerism. He did not smile. I had been prepared to a small degree; they told me he was receiving a new kind of treatment.

Shock treatment was a term I heard mentioned in whispers or under circumstances when I was thought to be out of earshot. My Webster's Junior Dictionary or World Book Encyclopedia had no mention of the term, so my imagination of its wonder and horrors was all I had to fall back on. As I looked at my uncle sitting there, inert as a plant, a picture entered my mind. There must have been a prolog imposed upon his memory perhaps after-the-fact. A stormy day with gathering clouds, winds reaching near tornadic force, his face pelted with sand and flying twigs. And then. And then the bold of lightning, entered his temple and stomped out a war dance deep into his brain. His body jerked from the force and his nostrils tried not to accept the acrid smell of frying flesh. He tried, but could not keep his eyes closed and the lights of the procedure room became intolerable. Finally, he released himself to the inevitable and relaxed his body into a state of unasked for, but welcomed catatonia

Uncle Legion motioned me to him; the others occupied with talk of their own. He whispered in my ear. His words have been stuck in my memory for all these years; no matter how hard I try I cannot forget them. When he finished he backed away showing the same smile he had presented upon our arrival.

We left Uncle Legion that day, his thirty-sixth birthday, and I never saw him again. At least not the happy, smiling Uncle Legion I left sitting in the visiting room. The day after our birthday visit, something went wrong with his treatment. The lightning bolt was too powerful or misdirected and its effect was devastating. On our next visit Uncle Legion had been relieved of all human responsibilities. He sat staring into space, showing no emotion whatever.

I will always remember the words he whispered to me. "I can't decide," he had said.

The look of puzzlement on my face prompted him to continue. "Whether I need to live."

In 1949, Uncle Legion completed his life on earth perhaps by his own will. Sometimes I picture him as he gives out his last breath. I can see the demons leave him and enter into a single large boar, just like I learned from the Bible story in Sunday School. Mostly though I think of Uncle Legion in happier days, before his collapse. Back when we played football in the backyard and I watched how fast he could run and how strong and direct he could pass the ball. And I remember how my dream was to be just like him in every way.

The Other Side of Legend

Billy the Kid
accepted the bullet
and the Act was complete.

Not the simple act—the precise moment
of a trigger pull—but that
composed of hundreds of choices
subtle and harsh,
understandable and baffling.

And with this acceptance
he forsook his future:
seeing horseless carriages and aeroplanes,
listening to sound from wax cylinders,
basking in the glow of an incandescent bulb.

Just outside
a bird startled by the shot
flew toward the east,
back to the beginning,
stopping only long enough to rest
in Dearborn and Dayton and Menlo Park
To rest and perhaps coo a regret.

How I Came to Leave Harper 1952

One of my grandsons in preparation for a school project asked me the other day about the place where I was born and raised and it got me to thinking, not so much about the time I lived in Harper, Mississippi, but more about the day I left.

I was born and raised in Harper. My parents were killed in an automobile accident on the way back from Houston when I was ten years old. I was taken in by my great aunt, Grace, an old maid who had been spurned by a lover in her younger years. I think this came to affect my life with her and ultimately my life in Harper. She must have resented my youthful face and body because she never missed an opportunity to label me as plain. Since she would not allow makeup in her house I guess I was a gray looking thing compared to the other girls my age. No doubt in my mind she made me feel ugly whether I was looked upon by others that way or not.

During my junior year in high school I took a job at the Harper Theater selling tickets. Night after night I sat entombed in the narrow ticket booth and was the subject of the ignoring eyes of my classmates as they came with their dates to view the latest feature.

My last night in Harper was a dreary one with low clouds hanging over the town. The streets were wet and the pink neon lighting on the marquee flashed upon the clouds sending an invitation to movie lovers as far away as Tylertown or Liberty. People jumped in their cars and trucks and made their way to Harper. When they arrived it did not matter what was playing; they had come to see a movie made better than it actually was by the enthusiasm of its announcement.

To say my job was my life was not exactly true. While I was confident, enthusiastic, and determined while enclosed in my ticket booth, I felt inept, shy, and unmotivated on the outside. Lonely and afraid, it was only my fantasies that sustained me. My job had a fringe benefit, free movies. I took advantage and saw almost every film that came to Harper. The love and kisses I dreamed of were not delivered to me, but to Doris Day, Hope Lange, or some other surrogate. This may be the only thing that made it possible for me to remain in Harper.

I liked going to the Harper Lake Baptist Church where I always arrived early enough to get the seat behind the column on the third row from the back. Once seated I stuck my head in the pew Bible or hymnal and tried to appear prayerful enough to avoid conversation with of the other churchgoers.

I had no real friends my age. Looking back on it I guess I dismissed those who offered fraternity, not out of haughtiness but to stay away from the perceived pain and disappointment any relationship seemed to offer. Above all, the thing I most feared and most desired, a romantic liaison with a man, was out of the question. Any dream involving such things was quickly snuffed out by my appearance in it. No doubt I lacked the quality that attracts others, but I must say a few people recognized a potential for beauty in my features. Once I overheard a woman who was visiting my aunt comment, "She could be such a pretty girl if she'd fix her hair and wear pretty clothes instead of them old Sears dresses." Whereupon my aunt responded, "Don't let her hear you say that. You'll just set her up for disappointment. I know what I'm talking about when it comes to disappointment." The friend continued, "Don't she never smile. She don't seemed to be blessed with no smiles at all."

The night I left the line at my booth was long. The feature had been much anticipated in Harper and some who couldn't wait had taken the train to New Orleans where they walked from the train station to the Sanger Theater to view it. Looking back at the crowd I felt a little shiver come up my spine. I had never performed before such a large audience and it disturbed me. I would have been all right if Jim Jinks had not been one of those in line. Jim had always been nice to me, nicer than most anybody in Harper. When he got to the booth and ordered his two tickets he smiled and asked how I was doing. I felt a little wave of enthusiasm, but this was quickly wiped away by Marsha Glimber, Jim's date and steady girlfriend. She gave me a look that pushed me back in my lonely corner. And then she had the audacity to kiss him right there, on the mouth, And he didn't have the control to resist and kissed her back. It was so bad the people behind them were yelling for them to move on. One person even suggested they get a motel room.

This sent me to a point lower than I had ever sunk to. I don't remember finishing my duty, but must have because when I came back to the world I was standing in the office of Mr. Schultz, the theater manager, holding the cash tray with the night's proceeds. He accepted the money and turned away with no comment other than a droned out, "Good night."

"Good night, Mr. Schultz," I replied as my eyes studied the awkward pattern in his linoleum floor. "Mind if I stay and watch the rest of the movie?" I asked this knowing it was one of my perks but felt the need to get his acceptance, I guess.

"Watch all you want, girlie girl. No skin off my nose."

When I entered the theater a night scene was in progress and the room was as dark as dark could be to my constricted pupils. I stood against a back wall and waited for my eyes to adjust and as I watched I felt my self slowly drifting out of the audience and on to the screen and into the plot of the picture. Bart Johnston was playing a World War II veteran returning to his hometown, some place in Nebraska or Iowa. It didn't matter that I had missed the first part of the feature; I slid right into the action feeling every emotion as Bart anticipated getting back to his old life. He told me as I sat on the darkened bus beside him about the girl he was coming back to. He had a job waiting. His family, well established in the community were waiting with open arms. Every now and then a disturbance in the audience would bring me back and I found myself standing at the back wall, but not for long such was the force of Bart and his fate.

Things turned dark for Bart and consequently for me too. Bart's girl—while he was away—had found another fellow, the job turned out to be less than he was promised, and his family gave no support in his effort to return to his old life. After several attempts to win his girl back he decided to fly the coop and begin a new life in a new city. As good plots allow he found a new girl, prettier than the old one; a great job with money and power; and in general a life full of excitement and promise.

The movie ended with Bart Johnston standing on the rooftop of his apartment building looking toward the heavens. He spoke no words, but the look on his face and the crescendo of the music as the camera reached for the stars proved the point that hope is there for the finding.

As I left the theater and made my way to my room in Aunt Grace's house, I experienced waves of hope and optimism intermingled with deep, agonizing lows of despair. At once I was praising God for all my blessing and then with no line of separation I found myself cursing my plight.

At the corner of State Street and Liberty Avenue, where a left turn would take me home and reestablish my life in Harper, I paused and looked upward. There was no music and the camera remained stationary. I felt no connection with the stars and my despondency became overwhelming. I fell to my knees in the dewy grass in front of the darkened post office building. I remember stretching my arms skyward toward the same stars Bart Johnston had looked upon. His victory was not mine.

"Oh, Lord, please," I cried. "Please, please, please." Each word louder until I was shouting.

No one came by. There were no witnesses that I know of. But I could feel the presence of every citizen of Harper as they watched my breakdown.

"You and you and you," I screamed, as I slowly turned—still kneeling—full circle pointing at invisible miscreants. Midway through my third rotation, I stopped abruptly, picked myself up, and straightened my garments.

Calmly I prayed, "Show me what to do dear God. Please show me the way." I suppose I was asking for a sign, any sign.

At that moment Mr. Schultz flipped the switch turning off the marquee lights delivering Harper into darkness. And in this darkness I stood, arms raised, patiently awaiting my fate. Lightning or deliverance, either would have sufficed.

Then there was light. The headlights of the Greyhound bus, just arriving in town and turning onto State Street, sent a beam upon me. Abruptly, without knowing why or even wondering why, I joined the bus as it slowly approached the station. Then, I was standing in front of Myrtle Mays, the ticket agent.

"Well, Shirley. What can I do for you?" Myrtle was obviously puzzled by my presence at her counter.

"A ticket to Jackson," I whispered.

"Did you say a ticket to Jackson?" She shouted, I guess in the way of announcing my request to the other passengers.

"Yes'm"

"Will that be a round trip ticket?" asked Myrtle her voice even louder than before.

"No, ma'am, a one way one please."

"Well what do you know? A one way ticket to Jackson," boomed Myrtle. "Well, one way is the best way I always say."

Several in the crowd laughed and I could feel their eyes upon me.

Myrtle handed me my ticket and just as I turned toward the departure gate, she got in her last dig, "Poor little thing ain't got no luggage a'tall. One way my foot."

"Hurry along, Missy," said the driver in the softest of tones. "Don't want to make me get behind schedule do you now?" His smile offered a happy transition from Harper to whatever lay ahead.

Almost as soon as I was seated the bus began its journey. I looked out the window at all I ever knew. Harper Food Store and Harris Drugs whisked by. I wondered if I would ever see them again.

In an instant, the bus was out of Harper and traveling north on Highway 51 on its way to my future. It was then I noticed the old man seated beside me. His hair and beard were milk white and his black clothes presented a sharp contrast. Night and day. Good and evil. His right hand supported a homemade walking stick and his left arm cradled a Bible.

He looked me over and sighed. "Do you know where you're a going, sister?" he asked in the manner of a revivalist under the fire of the spirit.

I did not pause and uttered my response, an answer I can hear myself uttering today, "Away. I'm going away."

Walking Home From The Harper Theatre (1954)

The movie was over at nine o'clock, but Jack stayed to see Doris Day sing "Secret Love" one more time. And as he walked home, he took the long way so he could develop his own arrangement of the song. He was composing as he passed the drug store where he had completed a shift as soda jerk just before the movie. Through the windows he could see the fountain where he had, a few hours before, scrubbed the sinks and ice cream box lids. The last customer was Lila Denson. She only wanted a Coke. Lila was the kind of girl he could go for. She was so well put together, both by nature and personal grooming. He couldn't help notice she was on the verge of filling out her lavender sweater.

Within the third block stood a bridge, called the overhead bridge. He had passed no one, seen no one since leaving Harper Theatre. He looked around to assure himself he was alone and began to sing aloud.

Below, the southbound passenger train The City of New Orleans, passed directly under him, screeching its way to a stop at the Harper depot. This was the train he had ridden home from Jackson many times. Some day, when he was older, he could go anywhere in the world and it would start by stepping on the porter's stool and climbing up into the passenger coach. He watched as ten or so passengers left the train and were met by friends and family. They carried their baggage and went directly to cars and trucks and the station was soon deserted.

The chorus of his song would have to wait. He had entered a block with houses and some of the lights were out. Mrs. Ellenwood's house stood dark and silent behind a jungle of shrubs and bushes. He once had a nightmare with this eerie house as the setting. In his dream, things reached out of the thick vegetation touching him with slimy, cold fingers. In the dream he could feel a scraping on his skin as he pushed his way into the house. The scene shifted and Jack stood in a room with a multitude of chests each with a dozen or so drawers. One drawer with a shiny silver handle caught his attention. Slowly he opened it. The drawer seemed to have no bottom just gray and murky walls descending into darkness. He leaned over and an unknown force pushed him from behind. He had awakened, wet with sweat and out of breath.

Once he had accompanied his grandmother when she visited Mrs. Ellenwood. He was surprised to find a warm and cozy interior, flickering flames in a large fireplace and the smell of freshly baked bread. This was how he imagined his brain. Deep inside loomed a peaceful, restful place. But he was rarely able to get there because of the thick and thorny growth on the outside.

Tonight as he passed the old house, he felt an atmospheric change of some nature, like the air around him had been sucked up and replaced with a cooler, damper vapor. He could smell the shrubs, an odor that proclaimed their fertility. He thought of Mrs. Ellenwood's granddaughter who lived in Memphis. She was about the most beautiful girl he had ever seen.

Next, he walked by a house where during all the daylight hours in all kinds of weather a boy sat in a wheelchair. The boy had some spastic condition and would yell out to Jack as he passed, "Hey, boy. Hey boy." That's all he ever heard from the porch. Sometimes the invalid boy's sister would be on the porch. She read romance magazines as she watched over her brother. The girl was four or five years older than Jack. Her manner of dress and choice of reading material led him to believe she was knowledgeable in the ways of the world. Was a romance with an older girl possible? He had thought through the pros and cons many times. Tonight the empty, silent porch caused a little shiver to run through his body.

In the next block the house of Sydney Davis, a girl from his ninth grade class, was dark except for a glow from the rear where there was a sort of patio, an uneven arrangement of concrete blocks left over from the addition of a garage. In front a forty-seven Buick coupe was neatly parked. It was the handy work of David Hemmingway. David had replaced the old engine and spent many evenings and Saturdays installing slick, black and red leather upholstery. Now, Sydney was entertaining David. Lucky guy. Sydney was quite a girl. He could really go for Sydney.

The lumberyard lay ahead. Walking past the lumberyard at night was about the bravest thing a boy could do. Someone or something could be lurking behind any number of lumber piles. Something that could leap out and crush a person before that person had time to watch his short life flash in front of his eyes; or confess his sins to God. There was this door, a garage door but much larger, that he had to walk past. It was broken in a way that did not allow a complete closing. A perfect place for an ambush.

As usual, he crossed to the other side of the road, as far as he could get from the opening. He thought he heard a shuffling sound. That was enough to make him run as fast as he could to the next street light, half a block away. As he ran he prayed for forgiveness. A general confession about not being good enough, but as it had been on his mind, he asked forgiveness for thoughts he had—thoughts of Sally Morris, Becky Wheeler, and Maryjane Pirkle.

It was on these walks home that he went through a painstaking evaluation of his life. There was truly something wrong with him. He liked nearly every girl he knew. Liked them and considered a future with them. That couldn't be normal. All the other guys seemed to settle on one girl at a time. But not him. They were all beautiful and desirable. But they were all inaccessible. He had never been on a date. Girls were friendly enough to him, but he knew they would reject his invitation to a movie and certainly they would not go to a dance with him.

On a hill across the road sat the house of his Uncle Marley and Aunt Minnie. Its peeling paint and screenless windows always caused him a bit of embarrassment. Uncle Marley was his smartest uncle. He had an engineering degree, but instead of going to a large city and working for a big company, he had chosen to come back to Harper and work for the highway department. No doubt it was because of Aunt Minnie, a slightly built woman who had no claim whatsoever to beauty. The fact that Uncle Marley, tall and handsome, had chosen such a homely bride had always perplexed Jack. None of the girls he liked were plain. And they were smart. Aunt Minnie never laughed at jokes or seemed to enjoy anything in life.

About a week ago, he found opportunity to talk alone with Uncle Marley. Since his issues were pressing hard on his brain, he blurted out his concerns to his uncle in one long diatribe. Marley, the smart one, had little to say.

"You're only fifteen. Things will work out. They always do."

The boy was sorry he brought it up. He should have known his uncle, who had chosen a woman as ugly and stupid as Aunt Minnie, could not have the insight and intellect to solve a problem so great as the one confronting a fifteen year old, heading for who knew what in life.

A block ahead his house, the only house he had lived in, was sitting to the back of a treeless lot. All vegetation except the grass that needed mowing twice a week had been cleared away. There could be no secrets in a house with such exposure. He could see the light in his father's room. His mother and father had slept in separate rooms since he could remember. Maybe it was because his father was so much older than his mother, about ten years.

His father, insomnia prone and restless, could be heard walking throughout the house all hours of the night. He taught English at the junior college up the road and he looked the part with his round glasses and ivy league clothes. Jack had often bumped into his father at night with his reading glasses hanging from his neck, gray bathrobe and leather slippers. He was always carrying a book of Keats, Yeats, Dickens or Hardy. Certainly his father would not be the person to talk to.

And his mother. She was so wrapped up in the Harper Garden Club, Ladies Home Missionary Club, and the P.T.A. There was no room for her to counsel and advise. Jack had always felt his mother thought she was a step or two higher than either him or his father. When it came right down to it, she was a snob. A snob who lived in an old house with an old husband and a son who was screwed up in the head. She had no license to qualify as one of the elite. But she was beautiful. Everyone thought so. He could see how his father had fallen for his mother.

He tried to open the door as gently as he could, but an unoiled hinge alerted his father of his arrival.

"Jack, is that you?"

"Yeah, Pops, it's me."

"It is I."

"Yeah, it is I. Such as I is."

In his room, he dressed for sleep. As he was climbing into bed he saw a volume of poems by W.B. Yeats. And inserted in the book was an envelope marking a certain page. He opened the the book and read:

> *I whispered, 'I am young,'*
> *And then, 'I am old enough'*
> *Where fore I threw a penny*
> *To find out if I might love,*
> *'Go and love, go and love, young man,*
> *If the lady be young and fair.'*
> *Ah, penny, brown penny, brown penny,*
> *I am looped in the loops of her hair.*
> *O love is the crooked thing,*
> *There is nobody wise enough*
> *To find out all that is in it,*
> *For he would be thinking of love*
> *Till the stars had run away*
> *And the shadows eaten the moon.*
> *Ah, penny, brown penny, brown penny,*
> *One cannot begin it too soon.*

He read it again and then again. How could his old father know what he needed? They rarely talked about anything, much less his young life. Maybe the old man had an insight greater than he could have hoped for. Maybe it was time to climb on the train, open the drawer.

Then he thought of Emily Moultrie. Emily had long blonde hair and wore it a different way almost every time he saw her. But it was her lips that intrigued him. They were full and looked as if they were made for kissing. Maybe he should ask her to go with him to the dance after the next home game. She usually came with a bunch of girls. He thought of what it would be like to hold her close and feel her warmth, smell her shampooed hair and well-placed perfume. That was all good, but that was only a part of it. He would be kind to her and give her everything she wanted. He would love her until the day one of them died.

Tomorrow, he would call her. Or maybe not. Maybe he should call Juanita Boardman. She was prettier than Emily. And she seemed to like him. Once she had told him she thought he had a great wit. Juanita would be wonderful. But it would be unwise to forget about Linda Moore. Linda would be a damn good choice.

His Minnie

She lived in a house with plastic curtains and artificial flowers.

Her voice was high-pitched, often scratchy.

And her perfume, loud and stifling, hung around long after she was gone.

He had trouble with the way she looked, frumpy and kinda thrown together and her hair was never the way he thought it ought to be.

She didn't understand half of what he said.

Even the little things that weren't all that deep and profound.

But, you know what, when she walked into a room and stood before him the thing that went around in his mind was Aaaah.

There was just something that kept him in the game.

Something like a force, but wispy and ethereal.

And everyday he wondered what it was.

Until the day he died he wondered what it was.

The Railroad Watch
1955

Gabe Saucier drew his last breath at 4:22 AM. The bed in which he lay, made of some lightweight metal with peeling white enamel, sat in room 6115 in the Illinois Central Railroad Hospital in Chicago. On admission to the cardiac clinic, doctors had determined his condition serious enough for closer observation. His journey to Chicago had been difficult and as he walked in the confusion of a distant city and allowed strangers to attend his medical needs, he was at first bewildered and eventually slipped into a state of utter despair. Attempts to remember why he was in a hospital bed turned to short flashes of recall leaving him at a loss to sustain mental pictures even of Ada, his wife and of his family. His greatest fear, dying alone, had slowly moved over him and now manifested itself in an overwhelming panic.

Beside Gabe on the bedside table lay his railroad watch. His last physical act was to reach for the watch, grasp it in his trembling hand, and hold it to his chest.

The hospital staff went through all the necessary steps when a patient dies. Within an hour Gabe's body was moved to the morgue and his belongings were placed in a cardboard box and labeled for delivery to his home in Harper, Mississippi. All so neat and impersonal. As cold as death itself.

This occurred on Tuesday, May 24. Less than thirty-six hours earlier Gabe and Ada stood between the depot and tracks waiting for the City of New Orleans. For months Gabe had resisted the local doctor's admonitions to go to the main hospital in Chicago. He needed special care and railroad insurance dictated the Chicago hospital as the only approved facility for such attention. He had finally given in when breathing became difficult and moving short distances required all the strength he could muster.

They held hands. Ada was there for him. There was nothing Gabe could have thought of that would have kept her away. She had spent the morning begging him to let her go with him, stay with him throughout his ordeal, hold him, somehow keep him from slipping away. Gabe had explained the hospital policy. She would have to find a room in a hotel and stay there alone. He would never permit this.

Church bells rang out, a call to morning worship. Gabe could sense impatience in Ada's twitching fingers and knew that as soon as the train was out of sight she would make her way over the bridge that spanned the tracks and down Pearl River Avenue to her church.

Gabe was impatient too. It suddenly occurred to him he was wishing his life away. The sooner the train came, the sooner he would be separated from Ada. It was almost laughable, this strange impulse to move on with life even with an unsure and less than promising future ahead.

The train could be heard, just out of view, as it raced toward the station. A miniature engine appeared and grew larger as the engineer slowed the big machine for its stop at Harper. Gabe knew all this. He had applied the same maneuvers a thousand times on the freight trains he engineered.

It was time to go. He gave Ada a hug and a quick kiss. He saw no tears in her eyes; her smile was full of optimism. Gabe knew she would hold it together until he was out of her sight. The porter grabbed Gabe's suitcase and pushed it up and onto the train. He helped Gabe up on the platform and walked with him into the car where he was to sit.

"I'll take care of your bag, sir," he said.

Gabe took his seat and saw Ada standing just beneath the window. She mouthed the words: I love you. He looked down upon her and studied each line of her face with no less attention than an artist mapping out a portrait, her brown hair now with an almost equal portion of gray, her fair skin no wrinkles showing at this distance, and her brown eyes still flashing a youthfulness that belied her age. Gabe nodded recognition of her love sentiment and tried to bring the right words to his lips. All he could do was send her messages of his love by keeping his eyes in hers as long as distance permitted.

Then Ada, and Harper were out of sight. But images of his wife tiptoed over and through the regions of his brain. Back went his thoughts, back to the beginning for his life in reality began with her.

The Tickfaw Baptist Church was celebrating the return of three members come home from the fighting in Europe. It was said this was the last war the world would see, the war to end all wars. President Wilson promised a new and bold plan to assure everlasting peace. Several young people from nearby communities had come to Tickfaw to greet the soldiers.

A spirit of joy and contentment filled the tabernacle located directly behind the church. The tabernacle, a simple structure, iron supports holding up a tin roof, was built with no walls, to allow open-air worship during the hot Louisiana summers. The floor was covered with sawdust. When Gabe looked up at the heavy girders supporting the roof he could almost hear the amens and hallelujahs from years of preaching and singing hanging there, lingering, unable to break out and ascend toward heaven.

Gabe spotted Ada as soon as she walked into the building. She was petite and dressed in a colorful frock, sky blue with a yellow sash. She seemed to Gabe at once confident and yet shyness could be seen in her eyes. Her eyes. That was what he carried with him from that first meeting and through the rest of his life. When he was sitting behind the furnace of the train's engine or even when he was lying beside her in the dark of their bedroom, he could feel her eyes. Dark, dark brown. A little bigger than they should be and shining, always shining.

When he tried to talk to her that night at the church, she was courteous but showed no sign of interest or acceptance. She had simply turned to her friends and walked away from him.

Later when they were better acquainted Ada told Gabe about her early impression of him. Her sister had spoken of him:

"Who's that good looking guy?" the sister asked.

"Do you think he's good looking?"

"Don't you?"

"Well maybe. He is tall and I kinda like his curly hair."

"Uh huh," said her sister. She then gave Ada a little poke in the ribs.

Later in the evening Gabe took his turn at the ice cream churn. When it was ready, it was Ada who brought forth the bowls and held them while Gabe scooped mounds of white goodness into them. Little was said but they both knew their lives were changed forever. Over the years they laughed about that night, each claiming it was the other who was first smitten by love.

Their wedding was simple, after a Sunday church service. Then family, friends and curious church members gathered in the tabernacle for cake and iced tea. There was no honeymoon trip. Gabe had remarked their honeymoon was never over because they didn't have to come home from it.

The time between the wedding and their first child went slowly and was filled with nights of promises, each trying to outdo the other with the intensity of their commitment. But the next three children came quickly. Ada confided to her unmarried sister, "Every time I turn around I'm expecting."

Gabe started out as a fireman, shoveling coal to fuel the trains of the Illinois Central Railroad, employment that made a move to Harper necessary. Their first house was too small for their growing family, but they made do.

Gabe was ambitious and good at his work. He was soon made engineer. In spite of his young age he commanded a certain respect among his fellow workers.

Now as Gabe sat on the train he watched familiar landmarks flash by. Barns and houses that he had used as reference to how far or near he was from home. He reached in the watch pocket of his pants and pulled out his gold railroad watch, a maneuver he had done so often while riding the rails. He remembered the day when he came home from a trip and found Ada in the backyard hanging clothes on the line. He came behind her, took her in his arms and held her close.

"Ada, baby. I need to buy me something," he said.

"What could you possible need, Daddy? You got everything you need right her on North Magnolia Street."

"Yeah, I guess I do, but I need a railroad watch. I have to be able to tell the time without asking some other fellow. It's getting embarrassing."

"How much does one of them watches cost, Gabe?"

He turned her toward him and held her by her shoulders. He often did this when he wanted to make sure she saw things his way.

"There's a guy who got to sell his. He's run into some bad luck with doctor bills for his wife and kids. He says I can have it for thirty-five dollars."

"Ain't that a lot for a watch?"

"Not for a railroad watch. They a cut above a regular everyday watch. We could find a way to cut back on other expenses."

"I can't see how, but I guess if you a railroad man you got to have a railroad watch."

Gabe came home from his next run with the watch. During supper that night he pulled the timepiece from its special pocket in his overalls and announced the time to the surprised kids.

"The correct Central Standard Time is now, right now, at this very minute . . . ." And he would give them the correct time. He provided this information several times during the meal. Each time Ada and the children laughed abundantly, bringing a high degree of satisfaction to their proud father.

Over the years Gabe held the watch above all his possessions. He took it in regularly for cleaning. When the jeweler could get to it right away, Gabe would wait next door at the barbershop until the work was complete. Once he had to leave the watch over night. During those hours he kept poking his fingers in the empty pocket in disbelief the watch was not there. The next day with the watch safely in his hands he swore he would never leave it again.

The train moved to the northeast, away from the freight route Gabe had traveled so many times in his career. He thought of long nights spent away from home, away from Ada. It was on those nights in small towns with rundown hotels and cheap beer joints that Gabe began to drink. At first it was now and then to be sociable, at least he had convinced himself it came about that way. In those early days he never drank while he was home, so Ada had no idea this habit had begun. But what started as a simple act of camaraderie became a debilitating condition, a condition he could not simply leave on the road.

When he began to stagger home from the dumpy bars that lined the street across from the train tracks, Ada took charge. She vowed to load up the children and go back to Tickfaw to live with her mother. This was all Gabe needed to drop his drinking. He stopped for several years.

The children came of age and the two older girls married local lads and started a life of their own. Then war that was not supposed to happen broke with a sudden furor. Ada and Gabe watched helplessly as one of their sons went to Europe and the other to the Pacific. Two stars hung in the window of the front room of their house.

After the war one of the daughters, her husband, and their young boy had to move in with Gabe and Ada. Though this was not unusual for the time, Gabe was not comfortable with the situation. He considered his son-in-law a failure for not being able to support his family in the way that he himself had done. Ada made him promise to be civil and keep his feelings to himself.

The hidden blessing for Gabe was the boy. They spent every minute they could together. The boy, they called him Jackie, was fascinated by his grandfather. He loved the stories Gabe told of growing up on a small farm on the edge of a Louisiana swamp. There were tales of snakes, six feet long with two-inch fangs and rattles so loud they could be heard a quarter mile away. And there was the two-headed calf born on a neighboring farm and the fifty-pound catfish that required a substantial slug on its head with the edge of an oar in order to land it.

Gabe knew the boy loved these stories but the thing he loved most was the railroad watch.

"What time is it, Pawpaw?" he asked several times a day.

Gabe never hesitated to announce the time.

The boy was assigned duties around the house, mainly yard work. Gabe gave him a dime for the Saturday matinee after he completed his work. Raking leaves was a year round job because some of the trees kept ugly brown leaves until the new foliage appeared in the spring. An old magnolia tree on the south side of the house provided a particular problem for the boy. The leaves did not fall year-round but when they were falling they fell continuously. Jackie was sent back time after time until the lawn was completely free of leaves. Gabe would throw his head back in laughter while the boy scurried around working for his Saturday dime.

One day the boy came home from school, fifth grade, and found his grandmother crying.

"What's wrong, Maw Maw?" he asked.

"Never mind, Jackie. Run along now. Go out and play."

Later Ada told the boy's mother Gabe had been arrested and was in the city jail. He had succumbed to his old drinking habit and the result was a fight. Another drunk had tried to talk him into selling his railroad watch for ten dollars. This outraged Gabe and he poked the guy in the eye.

The boy had never known anyone who was arrested and certainly had never thought this could happen to someone he loved and admired. He must have been devastated, must have dreaded facing his grandfather.

Later that day as Gabe was walking toward home, he spotted Jackie walking back and forth along the bank above the sidewalk on the side of the house. The boy appeared to Gabe to be looking for a way to escape the situation so Gabe signaled for him to come and meet him.

"Hey, Jackie. Know where I been? I spent the night in the calaboose. Right in the cell with three other men who had too much to drink. Know how bad that made me feel? Well it was real bad. Know how bad I'm gonna feel facing your grandmother? Pretty bad. Real, real bad. You run ahead and tell her I'm coming. Try to ease her into it. Can you help me out?"

"Yes, sir. I can try."

The boy ran to the house and told his grandmother that Gabe was on his way in.

"Oh, Jackie. He's home."

And she ran out to meet her husband and took him in her arms and kissed his face and neck. That night she cooked him a steak as big as the skillet and added extra butter and cream to the mashed potatoes and served pecan pie with vanilla ice cream.

Gabe knew the boy learned many things that day.

Gabe looked out the window of the northbound train. He reached into his pocket and retrieved his watch; he held it to his ear and listened to the measured ticking, music to Gabe, a song of home. From the train he saw land he had never seen before. The thought of his distance from home brought tightness to his chest. Riding in the passenger coach was a rougher trip than sitting in the engine. The tracks on this segment of his route were in disrepair; Gabe was jolted back to the reality of his journey. For the last ten years, maybe more, his health had declined. Early on, the doctor said it was Gabe's heart and prescribed digitalis and a diet without fat and told Ada to try to keep worry out of his life. The war was over, the boys were home and married and somewhat prosperous, the girls seemed happy in their marriages and the boy, his favorite grandchild was fast in running and adept in sports. Gabe had nothing to worry about. Nothing except the possibility of leaving Ada alone, uneducated in anything other than cooking and housekeeping. She couldn't even drive the car.

This is the thought that ran back and forth in his mind, through Tennessee and Kentucky, through the setting sun and into the night, and through the length of the state of Illinois.

The train pulled into Union Station in Chicago. Standing in the atrium of the Great Hall beneath the one hundred foot barrel-vaulted skylight, Gabe felt lost and alone among the scores of travelers. He scurried around asking this and that person directions and was shown where the taxis stood waiting, ready to deliver him to the Illinois Central Hospital. His admission to the cardiac clinic and subsequent hospitalization was a whirlwind of activity all beyond his control. This was new territory. Gabe had always felt he was in charge of life and the lives of his family, but here he felt as if he were speeding along the railroad tracks in an engine with no levers, gauges, or brakes.

Gabe lay in his bed; he felt he might already be dead, floating in some kind of purgatory, neither here nor there. The pain in his chest became more intense. After midnight on his second night in the hospital, the vice-like tightness compelled him to call for the nurse. She told him she would summon a doctor.

Hours later the doctor had not arrived. Gabe struggled for breath as his condition worsened. He reached for his watch, in a valiant show of will and made out the numbers. It was just after four AM. The watch was all he had. It was everything he had known, all the events of his life, all his family, all his friends. He placed it close to his heart as he took a final gasp of air and soaked in all the watch held, all the vibrations of his life, and carried them with him on his journey into the light.

Broken Crutches (1956)

This was the day we had waited so long for; the day when Elsie was coming home to save us. Through sleepy, bloodshot eyes I watched Grandpa make his way—hangover ridden and rumpled as a soldier returning from battle—down the back-hall stairs and into the kitchen. I had a hangover too. We had stayed up till two or three drinking Old Overholt with beer chasers, a combination that laid a heavy regret on the top of my brain.

"You okay, James?" asked Grandpa. My mother's maiden name was James and she had insisted that everybody address me by what I considered an appellation too formal for the town of Harper. After she passed on I made sure my friends called me Jim.

"Fine as kind," said I.

"You don't look right. Maybe you ought to go back to bed."

"And have to face getting up all over again?"

"Suit yourself." Grandpa eased out his words with an accent acquired from a life long association with rednecks and good ole boys, all drunks and ne'er-do-wells.

"Anyway I got to pick up Elsie at the train station in New Orleans. She gets in at three thirty."

"Well you don't want to be late. She'll eat you up, don't ya know?"

Grandpa spooned coffee into the basket of the old percolator. He made it harsh to my taste. He required harsh just like he needed pepper and hot sauce in a quantity enough to light up the tongue and throat of most people. He cracked three eggs into a bowl and beat them up with a fork. After shredding cheddar cheese into the mix he poured it into a skillet that he had used for frying six rashers of bacon. He left in all the grease. When the omelet was on his plate he added the Tobasco Sauce and pepper.

"Grandpa, you gonna burn your stomach out," I said.

"That'll be the day," said grandpa gruffing his voice into a John Wayne imitation. "You better move on if you're gonna meet that train. I'll take a good four hours to get to New Orleans. You got to go cross all them bridges, don't ya know? Bring us home another bottle of that rye."

My old forty-eight Ford almost knew the way across the swamps on its own, we had made the trip so many times. Saturday nights I used to play in a band down on Bourbon Street. That was right after the war. My regular job was in Harper at Thompson shoes, so I was driving across bridges and through small Louisiana towns every weekend for three or four years. My instrument is the fiddle and I still play some, mostly for my own amusement, but every now and then at church socials and such.

Elsie was coming home from Los Angeles. She went out there with the thought of becoming a movie star. And she had been in a couple of what they called B pictures. They showed in the Palace Theater in McComb. In one of them she was a cowgirl and the other a gangster's moll. She wasn't very good, at least that's what I thought. Coming home was a big defeat for her; I could tell from the way she told it in her letter.

Me and grandpa had been doing pretty good by ourselves; both of us got left by our wives. We drank too much, I know that. When Elsie is with us we're gonna have to change a little on the way we've been living. Clean up better and all. Maybe not drink as much. Probably be better for me anyway; I almost lost my job last week for coming in with whiskey breath. I swear it had been midnight since my last drink but Miss Thompson still could smell it. She sent me back in the storeroom to rearrange the shoes. She wouldn't let me wait on any customers all that day. Yeah, it'll be good to have Elsie home.

Elsie was Miss Harper High School her senior year. It wasn't just that she was pretty; her personality was the kind that immediately won over people—even strangers. I figured it was because she asked questions about the person she was talking to and showed she was genuinely interested in their well being. Every Sunday Elsie had stood in front of a group of young children and taught them Bible stories—Jonah and the whale, Moses and the ten commandments, Jesus and the loaves and fishes—holding their attention like they were watching *Snow White* or *Cinderella* at the picture show. I used to hear people say she was the all-American girl.

Then she was talked into entering that beauty contest and came in second for the whole state of Mississippi. And it didn't end there. She was discovered. An agent from Acme Pictures came all the way from Hollywood, California and was sitting in the audience. I guess they made her a deal she couldn't turn down.

Now she would be with us again. She would save us—me and grandpa—from perdition, eternal hell itself. I got a little despondent thinking about everything; how I graduated from college with high hopes, married the only woman I ever loved, and was blessed with two beautiful children. And how I had let it all fall right through my fingers like so much sand at the beach. I was feeling pretty low so I pulled off at Laplace for a shot or two of bourbon.

The Southern Pacific train was standing at the station when I got there. The passengers were climbing down with the help of porters. I thought I spotted Elsie toward the back of the train and started walking toward her. Then I thought it couldn't be her. This girl was all frumpy looking and seemed to be weaving a little, bumping into people who either ignored her or looked at her with aggravated glances. She saw me, tried to pick up her pace, lost her footing, and hit the pavement. I rushed to her and lifted her to her feet. She couldn't have weighed more that ninety pounds.

"Hello, brother," she said. "I'm gonna need your help. I'm gonna need your help real bad."

On the trip home Elsie didn't say more than things like, "I'm tired" or "It seems like only yesterday the last time I crossed this bridge." The sun was setting behind gnarled, sickly trees poking out of the swamp waters. I looked over at Elsie as she surveyed the depressing landscape.

"You know, Jimbo, I'm really counting on you and grandpa to help pull me up again. Back to what I used to be."

"We were kinda counting on you to pull us up."

Then we were both quiet and Elsie fell asleep until we pulled into the gravel drive and my dogs barked out a welcome home. Grandpa was sitting on the porch in his rocking chair. Beside the chair sat a glass half full of some liquid the color of diluted tea. One thing I was sure of, it wasn't tea.

Grandpa looked Elsie up and down, shook his head from side to side, sent a stream of tobacco juice sailing over the dead azalea bush by the steps, and sized up the situation with a single question.

"You get that Old Overholt?" he asked.

Who Says Dreams Can't Come True
1979

I don't know much, but I do know a liar when I hear one and Johnny Whitesides is a liar. Trying to tell me he had relations with Hilda when we were all in high school. I can't imagine any such event. If I were in my most imaginative state of mind, like when I made up a different ending to "Casablanca" (in mine she stayed); even then I couldn't come close to Johnny and Hilda. Not as ugly as he is. And he was even uglier back then, skinnier and acne infested, and he almost always smelled bad. No, that didn't happen about Hilda and all.

I think it's just that he knows how much I always liked her and wanted her to be my girl. I think he's just trying to get under my skin talking about such things. I mean look at who he married, Mozelle Banks. Just look at her, dirty fingernails and all. I'm telling you it just didn't happen.

Hilda was the prettiest girl in school, in my estimation, and was always real friendly toward me, and I don't mean in any sordid kind of way. Her daddy was a preacher, pastor of the First Baptist Church across town from where I lived. When I found out about her, after I moved up to high school, I switched churches so I could see more of her. She sang in the choir and I would sit close down front and she would smile at me all during the service.

Don't get me wrong. She had a steady boyfriend, and I know she was just being nice. But I do know she liked me some because when Buster, her steady, was playing football she would let me sit next to her in the stands, and under the blankets on cold nights, she would hold my hand. I never figured it out, but her hands were always warm as toast even on the coldest nights. I guess Buster never considered me much of a threat because he never said anything about me spending time with Hilda. He was big enough to break me in half if he wanted to. As I mentioned, he was a football player, a fullback, Mississippi All State in 1955 and 1956.

They never married each other, Hilda and Buster. She went to Garrison Bible College where she married a mathematics professor. He went to Mississippi State and married some girl he knocked up. But that's O.K. because when they came to our class reunion last month, they were real happy, all four of them.

Well, the reunion is why I'm into all this. I can't say I haven't thought of Hilda over all these years, but I haven't obsessed about her. It's just that when I saw her standing across the ballroom at the B.P.O.E. number 1798, where the reunion was held, I almost fell out at how beautiful she still is. It started me thinking. Thinking about how I should have pursued her back in high school. Holding my hand and smiling at me from the choir loft must account for something.

When I arrived at the reunion, I could see that the Bankhead twins, Veda and Vada had gone a little crazy with the decorating. The theme was stated on a piece of poster board on an easel at the door, "A Summer's Night Reunion." They must have strung a thousand Christmas lights—all white—in straight lines across the ceiling. And there were clouds of heavy cardboard covered with angel hair and glitter. An oversized moon hung mid-ceiling and was illuminated by a powerful spotlight. The result of all their industry was a brightness akin to a summer's day.

Through the glare I could see someone approaching. I recognized it was Johnny Whitesides by his walk. He always drags his feet. I get the feeling his footprints in the sand would look like two giant slugs had crept by on their way to nowhere.

"Hilda's here," said Johnny with a lascivious smile on his moon surface face. "And she's looking real good."

"That's great," I said looking around the hall trying to conceal my excitement.

"Yeah, good ole Hilda. Sweet lips Hilda. I can still taste those sweet lips."

"What? What are you talking about? Hilda would never kiss your ugly lips." That's exactly what I told him.

"More than that," said Johnny. "A lot more."

"Excuse me, but don't you think you ought to get back to Mozelle." I said with all the sarcasm I could muster.

"She'll be just fine," he said.

And with that, I turned my back and walked away from the little bastard. Excuse me but that's just what he is.

And that's when I saw her. She was standing in the middle of the dance floor introducing her husband to Buster and his wife. And she was gorgeous. In high school Hilda was pretty, but now she was beautiful. Her hair was lighter and shorter than she had worn it back then, but she had the same smile that she sent my way all those Sunday mornings. And her dress . . . I won't try to describe what that looked like, but take my word it was fantastic. I mean she looked just like a movie star.

And her husband looked old as Methuselah and was quite short—about a foot shorter than Buster. But I will say she was very affectionate toward him, patting his back and brushing his hair back off his face and introducing him with the highest amount of pride. I liked that even though it was directed toward him and not me. It just shows what a great person she is.

I moved closer and when she saw me, she turned away from the others—her husband included—and walked right up to me.

"Randy Miller." The sound of her voice sent a tingle through my nervous system giving me the feeling that miniature lightning bolts were shooting from my fingertips.

"Hey, Hilda," was all I could come up with.

And this is the part that really gets me. She put her arms around me and held me exceptionally tight and long, and kissed me on the cheek so very close to my mouth that the slightest move on my part, if I had been so inclined, would have had our classmates really talking. I could tell she was glad to see me, and you can see why it got me to imagining what it would have been like if I had won her away from Buster.

She took my hand into her hand—still warm as toast—and led me over to where her husband was standing. She introduced me as one of her dearest old friends and he shook my hand. His grip was surprisingly strong for someone who looked so old. He put me in mind of Pablo Picasso; nothing worse than an old virile runt.

We talked for a while and she told me about her grandchildren and her life in the city where they live. But I for the most part just answered their questions. "How did I like living in the old hometown?" and "How was my mother's health?" and "Was I seeing anyone special?" I did feel compelled to mention some of my successes at work though.

Then Hilda said, "Why do they have it so bright in here?"

"Well, you know how Veda and Vada are," I said.

But Buster did not say anything. He just walked over and unplugged the spotlight. The crowd, with the exception of the Bankheads, applauded loudly. And when Buster got back to our group, Hilda shot him a look that said more than thank you. I don't think Hilda's husband noticed, but Buster's wife did. Because she suddenly got in the mood to dance and literally pulled Buster all the way across the floor as far from us as she could.

And there I was just like it used to be, Hilda and Buster and then me, except now her husband was in there ahead of me too. I had to get away and the only thing I could think of to say was, "Will you excuse me? Nice to meet you. Nice to see you again, Hilda."

We parted with Hilda saying, "We hope to see more of you before the evening is over."

"We," she said.

That put me into a pretty deep gloom. She is we and I am just I and that's the way it's going to be. So I settled down at a table toward the back of the room, a table with no easy access where I could get my mind off my encounter with Hilda.

I could have had a chance with Hilda. You see, I was supposed to go to the same college as she; even went so far as paying the deposit or whatever they called it. But family circumstances made it necessary for me to start at the junior college just up the road from here. My grandfather could have and would have paid for me to go, but I figured I'd do it later, when things sort of stabilized with my folks. They stabilized all right when my dad's liver turned to jelly from years of boozing and he departed this earth after vomiting up most of his blood.

Then it was Mother and me. So, I dropped the notion of higher education altogether and set about trying to make a success of myself without that crutch. And I have done well. I'm considered very successful around here, managing both radio stations, AM and FM. I always, like I intimated, have had a good imagination, and I dreamed up all kinds of shows over the years. Match-A-Mate on the Air was responsible for twenty-five or more matrimonies in our community. And Dare to Dream, where we granted people's wishes on the air, was one of our most popular features. I had to be careful with that one, not to make idle promises, so we were very selective about who we had as contestants. I mean we could not pay for somebody to go to Paris, France or anything like that, but we could get people new Easter clothes and help pay for funerals and weddings and such.

I have had many opportunities with women, and if Mother's health had permitted, I probably would have married Avis Tucker back in 1972. Mother has had numerous maladies over the years, none of a fatal nature, thank God, but all debilitating to me as well as her. Avis and I got real close to marriage more than once and before she moved to Gulfport to manage a bigger motel, we were actually living in sin in one of her rooms at the Japonica Motel on a very regular basis. No doubt, I have had real good sexual experience. My life has not been wasted or anything close to that. It's just sitting there with the beautiful notes of "Earth Angel" coming from the sound system, I began wondering what it would have been like with Hilda.

We would probably live in Birmingham or Memphis or maybe Atlanta. And I would manage or even own a television station or two. Of course, I would double as program director, considering my imaginative qualities, and I have no doubt about the number of awards that we would win. That was easy to picture.

What was hard for me was the intimate part. When I started to think about Hilda and me together in a private kind of situation, I faltered. I could see her very clearly, just the way she looked that night. When I closed my eyes and reached out my hands, I felt her fingertips touching mine, ever so lightly but they were there. I smelled the scent she was wearing just as if she was sitting next to me. All of this just about took everything out of me.

But when I got to the part where we are so close to—you know—she turned away from me. That was devastating to think about. I could imagine Mavis and me together, I mean real clear. But Hilda...

But this is what really gets me. Right there with the voice of Fats Domino taking us back to "Blueberry Hill" and all the festivities of our fortieth reunion going on and more importantly with Hilda so close, I began to think about my mother. When I left her she looked so pale. She had been suffering with diarrhea for the last few days and the medicine she takes for it had helped very little. Just as I was walking out the door she asked me to help her to the bathroom. She was so weak I had to stand beside the toilet and let her hold my arm. All the while her eyes were trained on my face. I suppose to detect any sign of disgust. I am happy to say I kept a poker face throughout the whole ordeal. I'll never let her know what a burden she's been to me. I know it's not her fault, but she always seems to come down with something just before a big event in my life.

Johnny Whitesides. I know I shouldn't have given his comments a second thought, and it's not that I put any stock whatsoever into what he claimed. Because I knew it wasn't so. It was just that the most minute possibility that some freak like him had been successful with a one-of-a-kind girl like Hilda... and I, well, I just have let so many opportunities pass me by. That's what gets to me.

As soon as they announced the last song, and the Platters were just beginning to fill the hall with "The Great Pretender," I left. It was partly because of my mother's condition, but mostly so I wouldn't have to see Hilda again. I do so much better with her, in my dreams.

Like I said, I have had a good life. I am a deacon—at the same church where Hilda and I went. I have money in the bank. And I have, and I think this is very important, plans for the future. In fact, it's just a matter of time before I'll be forced to commit Mother to Ferguson's nursing home. I'm not hoping for this to happen, you understand. But it is inevitable. I love Mother dearly, but I am physically exhausted from all the care she requires, and I do plan to take a cruise when that unhappy day arrives.

Every Sunday, I review the travel section of the Times Picayune, focusing primarily on the Caribbean. There are always several cruises any of which will do for me: beautiful weather, beautiful scenery, and beautiful people. From what I've seen I'm almost certain to meet someone exciting on the boat; someone to have dinner with or even more. But at the very least, I feel certain that my dreams of Hilda will come easier when I can get a little distance between me and all my troubles.

COMEUPPANCE
1985

The walk back and forth to the cigarette ash receptacle was at least fifty feet. Josh had considered moving it down to a spot close to the chair where he had taken leave from his wife in order to smoke. The butt container was made of some heavy metal, lead he thought. Had to be lead, I'm not that weak. Margie knew he smoked; it wasn't that. What she did not know was he smoked two packs a day. He had made his way around the near-empty pool—six inches of water soaked leaves decaying at the bottom—to the depository four times, each time snuffing out his cigarette, but not until he had used it to light up again.

The chair outside the room was one of those metal tube, plastic strip devices that could be folded and stacked against the wall when not in use. The narrow walkway did not allow for both sitting patrons and others walking to and fro on their way to the vending machines. Josh had occupied the spot just outside his room for half an hour and intended to remain in place for at least another hour; so Marge would be sound asleep. It was easier that way.

There was a time when he would have been in the bed before her, waiting for her. This was before their last child had been born and he became—in his mind at least—expendable. His coaxing and attempts at romantic persuasion had turned to begging and finally a sort of disdain for her and eventually her body. Now the only result of finding her awake was a summary of his faults and weaknesses delivered with a sharp tongue from a memory that would shame an elephant.

Josh had tried to convince himself he was keeping a cigarette going to ward the bugs away. But he knew that was a lame excuse. Besides it wasn't working to that effect. Large moths dove past the flickering neon lighting that lined the eaves of the porch. He looked at his bare arms. The skin, in the gray lighting appeared to him to be the skin of a dead man; a man pulled from a pond or lake after a week of soaking in stagnant waters. He was clearly deteriorating and the neon merely brought out the truth. Maybe if he gave up smoking, and Pabst, and started to exercise and diet Margie would turn warm toward him again. Fat chance.

Next morning they were on the road again, on their way to the reunion in Harper. Marge sat in the passenger seat as close to the door as possible. He drove while sipping coffee and munching on the sausage biscuit he had collected at the motel's free breakfast buffet. Crumbs accumulated in his lap.

The trip was Margie's idea. She wanted to see old classmates, one in particular, Darlene Watts, nee Parcel. Darlene appeared on a regional TV show and had published a number of cookbooks. Josh had resisted, but as usual gave in to his wife's persuasion. Persuasion without reward, only consequences for refusal. It was the list of attendees that turned his mind away from the pleasure of renewing friendship and the camaraderie of old friends. Wilber Newman was coming.

As he drove along Josh thought of an October morning in 1952. That day television reception was particularly good. It seemed to be better in the fall for some reason. *The Today Show* from New York was a morning ritual in the Miller house. Harper was a hundred miles from the WDSU studio so an antenna stretching sixty feet into the air was necessary for any reception at all. Some mornings, viewing became downright irritating with snow and static breaking through the broadcast at the worse possible moments. Today there were no interruptions. Eisenhower, the Republican candidate, seemed to be moving toward the presidency. Commercial breaks consisted of the Channel Six logo in deference to the New York content.

Josh's father left for his work in the railroad shops in McComb before his wife and children awoke. He was unaware of Dave Garraway or any of the early morning personalities. Daddy, as he was called, showed no interest in politics. His main concern was the weather. When he was a boy he had been caught in a storm and pinned against a mailbox for a few minutes. Minutes that imprinted a fear of bad weather and the potential for bad weather deep into his brain.

Josh's mother scurried around the kitchen, scrambling and frying breakfast for her three boys. Josh was the oldest and did okay in his tenth grade work. The younger boys, Dick and Charlie, struggled to make passing grades at Harper Junior High. They were both seventh graders, Charlie had been required to repeat his fourth year.

"Mom. I have to tell you something," said Josh.

"What is it, sweetheart?" His mother's back was to him as she stood at the stove.

"I've got to stay after school every afternoon this week."

"For what?"

"There's this new boy, Wilbur, who came from Selma, Alabama. Mrs. Winslow heard me call him Fat Wilbur."

"Why did you do that?"

"Because he's fat," said Josh. He tried to add a little puzzled affect to his voice.

"Hmmm," said his mother.

Later on the way to school Josh caught up to Wilbur and shoved him against the brick wall on the side of Harper Drug Store.

"You got me into trouble, Fat Wilbur," he said.

"Sorry," said Wilbur. "Next time ask me first and I'll tell you what to say; how you need to address me in order to stay out of trouble."

"Fat Ass," said Josh as he gave a little jab into Wilbur's belly.

"Your observation astounds me. I wish I had your powers to see things as they are. Maybe then I would be able to see how stupid you are. But alas, I only see you as immaterial."

"Whatever," said Josh.

That evening Josh arrived home later than usual. The football team had been forced into a longer practice, the result of poor play in the last game. When he walked into the dining room there sat Wilbur. He was wearing a tie for heaven's sake. Josh turned abruptly and hurried into the kitchen.

"Mother!" he pleaded. She answered with a look that showed no room for any movement in his direction. The dinner was uneventful, at least that what his memory told him.

Josh and his wife arrived in Harper right after noon. Margie's parents had moved to Orange Beach and his were deceased. A stay in a motel was necessary. A block of rooms had been set-aside for the reunion group at the Holiday Inn in nearby McComb. Margie had insisted they stay there. She said she was sure that's where Darlene would be staying. Josh liked to stay in motels with a number in their name; they were cheaper.

They arrived early Friday afternoon in plenty of time to get to the first activity at the country home of one of their classmates. Margie had shopped for both of them the week before the reunion and laid out her choice of clothes for Josh.

"You got to look nice," she said. And don't be smoking so much. Nobody smokes anymore. Nobody but you. Remember to stand up straight and hold in that belly. Take some pride in yourself."

"Right," said Josh. "That Wilbur guy is going to be here. Sure hope I don't have to spend a lot of time around him. We never got along too well. They say he's made a lot of money out there in Colorado where he lives. I'm in no mood for a gloating fool"

"Who's they?" asked Margie.

"I just heard it. That's all."

On the way to the party Josh pulled into a carwash and pushed the deluxe setting as he entered the shed.

"Nothing's gonna make this old car look good," said Margie.

"Whatever," said Josh.

When they arrived several people were already out by the lake, drinking beer or cokes. Margie spotted Darlene surrounded by several of the women attendees. She hurried to join the group. Josh checked out the food. Crayfish. "I hate crayfish," he mumbled.

Josh looked over the crowd. No Wilbur. "Maybe he won't get here in time for this even," he thought. "Maybe he won't come to the reunion at all." But just as the relief that comes with the avoidance of a bad situation was sinking in, Wilbur stood before him trim and muscular. Wilbur held out his hand. His grip was firm and caused Josh to grimace a little.

"Oh, Wilbur. You caught me off guard. Do I still call you Wilbur?"

"What else?" said Wilbur.

"I don't know. Seems like everybody prefers to be called something different from what they were called in high school. A shorter name. Seems like it anyway."

"No, I'm still Wilbur. How have you been Joshua?"

"It's Josh now. Just plain ole Josh."

"How's it going, Josh?"

"Good. I reckon everything is good," Josh began to look around for some way out of his discomfort.

"Where you live now? I heard you were in Kentucky," said Wilbur.

"Was. I got transferred to North Carolina a couple of years ago. We like it there. Not that we didn't like Kentucky. We did. But we like North Carolina too."

Josh took his handkerchief from his back pocket and wiped his brow.

"Are you hot?" said Wilbur. "The breeze off the lake feels good to me."

"I'm okay."

Josh looked down and saw Wilbur was wearing an old pair of loafers. They were polished to a shine but were obviously several years old. He looked up and saw standing before him a man in incredibly good shape. Before he could stop himself Josh blurted out, "Do you work out?"

"Some," said Wilbur.

"I heard you were in Colorado." It was then that Josh noticed the tear at the top of Wilbur's pants pocket.

"Yeah I moved there right after Mississippi Southern. Been there ever since."

Wilbur's wife joined them. She was pretty enough but no raving beauty. This surprised Josh because he had been painting a picture of Wilbur's life in Colorado. He had considered a fat boy going off to college and gaining the discipline that accompanied maturity. A fat boy who was now in the best of condition and would probably be considered handsome if Josh allowed himself such an observation. Josh just presumed a guy like the one Wilbur had turned into would have a platinum blonde with a low cut dress revealing her enormous breasts. Instead Wilbur's wife, who was introduced as Sara, was merely attractive. She was plainly dressed but had a confidence that held her head high and provided short, concise answers to questions.

"You from Colorado?" Josh was struggling for conversation and that was what he came up with.

"Originally from Ohio. Moved out after college and met Wilbur there. Good to meet you Josh. Do you mind if I steal Wilbur for a minute? One of the guys wants to say hello. I'm sure we'll see a lot of all you this weekend. Come on, honey, people are asking about you."

As the couple walked away Josh could see their relationship was solid. They adored each other. The way he looked at her. The way she looked at him.

A couple of the other guys smoked and along with Josh found a spot behind an old work shed out of the view of the others. The talk was all about Wilbur. Josh learned he had made a fortune in the natural gas business. He had also written a novel that stayed on *The New York Times* bestseller list for a number of weeks. He was writing another. His wife taught English at the University of Denver and they had three girls. Three beautiful girls. This is what was reported during the smokes.

Later as Josh lay in his bed he listened to the light snoring of Margie, more like a moan, almost like the moans he once brought about when they lay together. And he thought of Wilbur. Wilbur and his pretty wife. A wife who looked at her husband like Nancy Reagan looked at Ronnie when he was speaking to the nation. Wilbur and Sara lying together; no need for two double beds in their room. There would be gently kisses. And as their kisses became more passionate . . . . Josh shifted in the bed looking away from Margie.

"I can't deal with this shit," he said aloud.

He reached for his cigarettes. His pants were hung over a chair with the room key in one pocket. He threw them on. His T shirt would suffice on such a warm evening. Gently closing the door he made his way to the side of the motel for a few smokes.

The next morning the group was scheduled to meet for breakfast at a local restaurant. Josh feigned illness. Margie was aggravated but her desire to see more of Darlene was stronger than her need to control her husband and she left him to his own misery.

His thoughts came swiftly and bounced from his high school years to last night's encounter. They were all about Wilbur and his idyllic life. Damn him. He ended up with everything and I got the leftovers. I married the cheerleader, but he got the prize—the real prize, cream of the crop, top of the list. But what really nailed the nails in his hands and plunged the spear into his side was one simple reality. Wilbur just didn't care what people thought. Damn it. Wilbur was above all that.

The note was simple and to the point: CALLED HOME ON BUSINESS.

Josh had made a decision and he was sticking to it. No more of this stupid reunion crap. He would deal with Margie later. She would be outraged at having to drive home alone, but what's the worse that could happen, she could kick him out? So what?

He gathered his things and called for a cab to take him to the train station. The train was not due to arrive for hours but he saw no need to remain in the motel where enclosed in a drab room he would be left to brood away the time. He needed to be outdoors. Besides he could smoke all he wanted outside the station.

There were two things he hadn't considered. First, Margie would return and find the note before he boarded the train. And he certainly did not expect Wilbur to be concerned about him and his illness. And that Wilbur would come to the room to check on him and Margie would spout out her disappointment of his leaving. When Josh looked up from his thoughts Wilbur was standing before him.

"You need to come back. There's a lot I have to say to you," said Wilbur.

"No need. You win. No need to say more. I got everything I deserve and more. You don't have to explain that to me."

Wilbur had a puzzled look on his face. "You don't understand. I wanted to thank you. That's all. If you guys hadn't been so hard on me I may not have got my act together. Over the years I've thought of you and some of the others who thought they were giving me a hard time. I'll admit I didn't like it at the time. But as I grew older I remembered we were just kids. Acting like kids. The net result—what ever your motive—was positive. I got to college and began to take care of myself. I worked out every day and studied hard at night. I did not want to be Fat Wilbur all my life."

Josh sat looking at his new shoes. Then he looked at Wilbur's shoes, the same old loafers from the night before. That dinner thirty years ago, his mother's attempt to heal, has no effect. They had continued to treat Wilbur like crap until the day they all left for college.

Josh considered what he could say to provoke a sock in the face? He could recover from a broken jaw; a missing tooth could be replaced. But this kindness shit could hover over him forever. He could think of nothing to say to that effect.

Wilbur spoke, "Come back with me. That is if you can really get out of the business thing at home. I want you to tell my wife about your mother's good cooking and your dad's fascination with the weather. Those are the things I remember about you. I'll never forget the stories your family told that evening I had dinner at your house. You had a great family."

Josh stood and reached for his suitcase, but Wilbur already had it in hand and was headed to the car. Josh followed. What else could he do but follow?

Forgetting Misty
1989

"I'll not come back again." Those words have passed my lips a thousand times and each time I meant them.

But I am back at Harper Lake sitting alone in my old car, top down, watching the reflection of a near-full moon bouncing on the rippled water. An intermittent breeze, soft as a mother's kiss, cools my face and hands. Between the gentle gusts I hear the oak leaves changing colors, a sound between the smoothness of September and the rustle of November. I think I detect Misty's perfume mixed with the autumn aromas.

The last time we were here, over twenty years ago, we parked in this same spot and I told her of my love for her. She held me close and accepted my kiss, long and deep.

The moon was, I believe, the same moon as this night, approaching fullness. I could see her blue eyes, gray in the moonlight, as she told me of another love, a better choice. She had met him in college. He was from Jackson, an all around guy, the kind who is captain of the football team and senior class president. His family was in that elite group known as the Jackson 400. He had money and a promising future. They were to be married in January.

But she said she would always love me in her special way.

Then she was gone.

Sometimes I see her, in her Volvo wagon when she visits her mother. I'm so thankful she lives eighty miles away.

I'm doing better. Some days I don't think of her until mid-afternoon or later. But then I feel a guilt not unlike the one I get when I wake in the middle of the night and realize I have forgotten my prayers.

A jeep has passed a dozen times. I suspect it's a couple of high school students, urgently looking for a place to park. I start my engine and leave my place to them. They may have important things to say.

I say aloud, "It's time to move on." I say it again, louder, as if the volume will improve the chance of my adherence.

"I'll not come back again."

Harper Lake

It's not a big lake,
just over a hundred acres,
but its place in our lives is enormous.
In picnic areas on the north and east shores
we have family reunions, class parties and church picnics.
This is during the day.

At night the lake takes on a different color.
The song of birds is replaced with the chirp of crickets.
The lure of the waters changes from the familial to the sensuous.
Lifelong commitments are made here.
Promises near impossible to keep.

I often come to the lake at night
stalking old memories,
trying to get past that one moment
twenty years ago
when happiness turned to perpetual gloom.
Nighttime provides no resolution.

Today, in bright sunlight I sit by the lake
and consider its significance.
I am calm and content in its presence.
I do not want to leave its shore to complete my day's work.
The warm light brings a clarity, logic to my thought.
Harper Lake sits still, seems trivial.
When you think about it,
it's only several million gallons of water.
Water not even fit to drink.

Kichwa Kubwa
1992

Jimmy Langsdale came back to Harper after a few years up North. He had been working for the St. Louis Zoo. This is one of the stories he brought home with him. It tells of him being an observer while doctors at the zoo were working on a Lion with a toothache. They preformed a root canal and Jimmy, who has a vivid imagination, told of all that was going on in the lion's head while the anesthesia was at work.

I can hear them. I mean I can understand their words. They think I am without intellect, basing this misconception on the smallness of a particular portion of my brain. And they are the ones who hold the microchip in such regard. I would tell them, if I had been blessed with vocal chords delicate and intricate like theirs.

Today, they took me on an excursion; a mere errand for them, but for me an adventure. This is true, in spite of the fact that I was taken for medical reasons. My tooth. It has been aching for days affecting my disposition to the point of bringing their undivided attention to my welfare. They say I need a root canal. They claim it is a gift not available to lions in the wild. I am lucky they say. I say if I had been born out of captivity, I would not need their dentistry.

I have always known I did not belong here, even before I heard them say it. A lot has been programmed on my genetic chip.

The truck arrived right on time. When I felt the familiar sting in my right hip I calculated the time of its arrival. Not in minutes as humans would, but in a more precise and natural chronology. The sting always brings with it a mellowing of my mettle. You see, my programming tells me to stand my ground, to attack any intrusion into my territory.

I mustered a muffled roar and heard them discuss the possibility of my arousal during the procedure. One of them describes the scene: the nervous dentist reaching into the numbed jaws of death and the numbing subsides and the jaws slam and the operator is maimed. They all laugh. I take no comfort in the fact that they have no more respect for each other than they do for me.

I don't remember the ride, but the surgical aromas in my new surrounding bring me close to sobriety. Still I hold little regard for my fate.

I feel the mask on my face and breathe in the sweet fumes of sleep. Then, nothing. Wait. What is there? Straight-ahead and—as I look—in all directions there is a greenish veil. I stand with the tentativeness of a newborn. With great difficulty I stagger toward the division. Its color begins to brighten causing me to quicken my pace. Sounds, vague and haunting call to me. When I reach the curtain, a push against it with my head reveals its solidity. It seems impenetrable, but I am compelled to break through. As I struggle it becomes evident that my will is the determinant of the wall's rigidity. Faculties heretofore unknown to me surface and abruptly I break through.

It is dawn. The green pastures of the Mara lie to the east and ahead of me. From the west comes the water scent of the Mara River. I know this is the land from which my mother was taken. It has been the inspiration for stories—didactic and entertaining—that she and the others who came from the old lands presented to us captive-born. It is also well marked on my genetic chip.

The green plain is populated with herds of wildebeest and zebra. Their black and white and gray stands out in the midst of the blue sky, the various greens of the grasses and trees, and the purple mountains. They are headed for a rocky ridge just before an acacia forest to the north. It is the dry season and their objective is the spring fed streams of the marsh. Making sure to stay in the tall grasses, I pursue them.

As I reach the reed beds of the Musiara Marsh, I stop. There are others. Lions. Moving into the open I reveal my presence. They come to attention as if calculating my purpose. My demeanor is confident, for fear occupies only a tiny speck on my chip. My stride speaks of fraternity, but borders on superiority. I am older; my mane is full and heavy compared to the two males before me. They smell of family. I allow them to approach and sniff out my characteristics. They seem impressed with my makeup and nod an acceptance of my intrusion.

I learn that they are nomads, cousins, only a month turned out of their birth pride. They wander the plains honing their hunting and fighting skills in preparation for dominating a territory of their own. With them is a lioness, sleek and maneless, forced form her pride because of a lack of prey in the territory. Too little food for too many members.

They call me Kichwa Kubwa—big head in the native, human language—because of the fullness of my mane. The young males beseech me to lead them; to help them establish a territory. They are impatient to find a pride with older lions, to oust them, and assume control. They are willing to recruit other nomads to join them in forming a new domain. They yearn for reproduction with all its sensual and progeny rewards.

I speak for patience. I disdain the need for set territories, telling them to make the most of their freedom. They do not understand my thinking. I see no need to bring up my former captivity.

The approach of a herd of wildebeest transforms our communication to signals of the hunt. The stalk begins. Low to the ground, we slink toward our unsuspecting prey. One of the hoofed creatures catches our scent. His snort sends a wave of panic through the herd and a mass exodus ensues. I spring to the chase and quickly overtake several slower and weaker members of the group. Defying all my natural tendencies I pass by them. They will not do for my first kill.

I spot a large, muscular male and leap for him, latching my sharp claws deep into his hips. With a mighty surge of power I twist to the right bringing the wildebeest to the ground. The lioness arrives and I allow her the kill. My nature has been affected by my captivity and it will take several hunts to awaken my instinct for killing. The young males have each made a kill and we sate ourselves with the bounty.

Later, with the sun high in the sky, a hazy stillness covers the plain. We lie among the shaded rocks, yawning our satisfaction. We talk of the day's hunt and of those to come. A warm breeze flows over my back and ruffles my mane. I can smell the scents of my kinsmen intermingled with wet and dry aromas of the marsh and plains. The lioness circles me twice. I show no sign of acceptance or rejection, but I do welcome her obvious adoration. She takes a place on a rock some distance away.

I am tired. The excitement and toil of the chase has caught up with me. I know I must sleep to prepare myself for the night stalk, but I do not want to give up the remembrance of the day.

I can hear the young males. They are speaking of me. "Kichwa Kubwa," they say.

It is morning and I fight for the waking that will bring another day of freedom on my plain. Slowly and sorrowfully, I become aware of my enclosure. No free run, but hard barriers greet my return from the night. A feeling dismay overwhelms me.

One day of freedom among all the days of my slow imprisonment is all I will be allotted. One day to romp the grounds that are rightfully mine. One day to experience the camaraderie of my African brothers. And that day has passed.

Old Leonid approaches to inquire on my recovery. I tell him of my adventures and my dismay at its completion.

It is his wisdom that reveals the true gift of my journey.

"It's about remembering," he says. "It is not the doing, but the memory of the deed. You can surely return at any time."

He is right. Now, if you pass my confinement and you see me pacing the boundaries, I am walking the Mara. My roar into the night is a summons to my cousins on the plain. And when you see me standing tall behind all the barriers, you witness the proud and powerful presence of Kichwa Kubwa, Lord of all Africa.

The Call of Old Ways
1995

The lottery ticket vibrated in the pocket of Vernon's blue blazer. Not exactly a vibration, more a burning sensation leaking through his coat lining, across his stiffly starched shirt, and onto his chest. A reminder of sin? He felt its presence minutes after depositing the ticket in his pocket and he felt it now as he swayed back and forth with the MARTA train's movement.

Vernon had prided himself on his ability to resist gambling and such temptations. But the sign with $87,000,000 in large red print called for him to return to his old ways. And the others had egged him on. "Nothing ventured, nothing gained," one of them had said. "Think of what you could do with that much money."

It reminded him of the joke or parable or whatever about the woman who agreed to sex for a million dollars, but was incensed when the solicitor requested the same act for twenty-five bucks. "What do you think I am a common whore?" she admonished. The man responded, "We have determined what you are, now we are quibbling over the price."

"It's the same thing," he thought. If shooting craps is a sin, then so is participating in a multi-million dollar game of chance."

The other salesmen had taken earlier flights out of Atlanta while he stayed behind to attend the services at the Peachtree Way Baptist Church. He had promised Marie and she would be expecting proof in the form of a church bulletin. During the service he felt the ticket in his pocket and came close to pulling it out and holding it up to the congregation as a confession of his fall to the power of the devil. Instead he sat still in his seat only moving to blot wet eyes with his handkerchief.

Since Marie had entered his life and brought with her a reliance on the grace of God, his missteps took on new relevance. Before, his attraction to and success with women had been no more than a badge of manhood—something to brag about to co-workers. After Marie, these trysts were sins, vile and corrupt, necessitating painful contrition. These bouts of guilt were like hangovers only they lasted for weeks or sometimes months eating at his insides and making him swear to himself and to God that they would never happen again.

But they had. That is until the ultimatum. Marie had been in a psychic sway when he arrived home from a trip to Memphis. She claimed she detected a particular scent of perfume that was not hers. She said he had guilt written all over his face. Her certainty broke him down. He confessed everything and answered her demands for details. He babbled out information in vivid description as if he were composing a cheap novel. She sat across the den looking directly into his eyes. When there was no more to reveal he came to her and she allowed his head in her lap, where large tears soaked through to her skin.

Her forgiveness involved lovemaking, after which they held each other and exchanged vows of attachment and devotion. She told him gently that there would be no more chances. He swore he would not stray again. And for her part to assure his fidelity Marie insisted he take a territory that had opened in her hometown of Harper, Mississippi. This move diminished opportunity, opportunity to move up in the company and provided Marie with the ability to keep him in a straight line.

The Marta train pulled into the station at the Atlanta airport two hours before his flight. As he walked toward the security gate music from cool, dark bars beckoned him to enter and fraternize with the weak and insecure characters that resided there. He knew better. Drinking, for him, led to other things. Things that got way out of control. That time in Montgomery it was just two beers and the next thing he knew he was in Anita Perkins' bed.

As he diverted his eyes from the Congo Room and its summons, he recognized the woman who stood across the corridor staring at him. She had been his seatmate a week ago on the flight from Jackson. They had talked of her position as principal of a school for exceptional children and of his career with a pharmaceutical manufacturer. She was unmarried and in his estimation much in need of companionship. Not that she was unattractive, only selective. She had spoken of her last relationship with humor, but Vernon could feel the hurt in her voice. He perceived her as a sure thing.

"Hello again," said the teacher.

"Hello to you. Headed back to Mississippi?"

"Yes, but my flight has been delayed. This happens to me every time I fly. Are you on your way home?"

"Oh, no. I'm off to Charlotte. Another meeting."

The teacher seemed interested and Vernon sensed opportunity. "My flight is over an hour off." Then quickly, awkwardly, "Would you like to get a drink?"

"Oh, thank you, but I think I'll go on out to the gate and go over some of the papers I collected at my conference."

She reached for his hand, shook it, and turned and walked away. Vernon stood in disbelief. But his dismay soon became acceptance, then gratitude. Divine intervention had saved him from another transgression. "Thank you, Jesus," he said.

As he boarded the plane, he reached in his pocket and felt the ticket. "Oh, God. I should have dumped this thing. Forgive me."

His seat was over the wing. Someone had once told him it was the safest place on an airplane. He thought of the woman in the airport, realizing he would have drunk alcohol with her and would have tried to make arrangements to see her back in Jackson. He knew he would have carried a relationship with her as far as she permitted.

As the plane taxied out for take-off Vernon squirmed in his seat. He felt an unfamiliar panic. The weight of his sins might be too much for lift off. He closed his eyes and tried to think of green pastures and herds of horses and waterfalls.

The 727 struggled to its prescribed altitude while Vernon struggled to keep his mind on good things. He thought of waves softly washing sandy beaches and cool summer nights in the Smokies. He opened his eyes when a stewardess tapped him on the shoulder and offered him a drink. The first thing he saw was her breasts. "Holy Shit," he thought.

"I don't drink," he said as he examined his shoes.

His relief at the successful takeoff turned to near euphoria. He extracted the lottery ticket from his pocket and looked it over as if it were a moon rock. He read the numbers aloud. "Seven, twenty-two, forty-two, eighteen, one, and the super ball number, twelve." The man who sat beside him looked up from his magazine and said, "As good numbers as any. Good luck."

"Oh, thank you. I don't expect to win. I just succumbed to the $87,000,000 sign. It's my first time to play. I'm really opposed to gambling."

Vernon turned to face his seatmate and saw a man of seventy or more years. His hair was full and white as milk and he wore the uniform of a clergyman.

"Are you a priest?" asked Vernon only an instant before realizing the foolishness of his inquiry.

"Episcopal," said the priest.

"And you don't think its wrong to buy a lottery ticket?"

"Right, wrong. They get mixed up sometimes. I guess one must look at the consequences of an action before making assumptions of guilt or innocence. Who have you hurt by buying this ticket? Did you deprive a child of food? Did you break a promise, to yourself or another? And most importantly what will happen should you win?"

"What do you mean?" asked Vernon. He felt the weight of a new concern.

"Many who have won have had their lives changed, not for the better. Lawsuits, divorces, estrangements, and the like seem to be commonplace among the winners. You should think about what you will do if you are, shall we say, the lucky one."

"I would try to do the right thing. I'm sure I would try."

"Are you married?" Vernon nodded and the old man continued, "What will happen to your wife? How will it change your life together? And children, do you have children?"

"Two," said Vernon. "A boy at Ole Miss and a girl at Duke. The money would take care of their education, that's for sure."

"But how would it affect them to suddenly be the children of rich parents? Would this make them better people? Don't you think that is the ultimate question in most issues: how will any choice we make affect our relationship with others and with God?"

The priest turned abruptly, his sermon complete, and closed his eyes. Vernon presumed he was praying but soon the rhythmic rise and fall of his chest indicated that he was asleep. Vernon stared at the numbers on the ticket, looking for some significance: the date of his marriage to Marie was the eighteenth, they had been married for seven years, his son Bobby was twenty-two, he was forty-two, and he had given up the promotion to district manager for his company twelve months ago. What about the one? Could it stand for won? That's silly. It's all foolishness. The numbers mean nothing. The chance of winning is one in a hundred million. Much more likely to be struck by lightning.

The pilot announced the descent to Charlotte and Vernon stuffed the ticket in his pocket and began to straighten himself for his arrival. When the plane stopped, Vernon assisted the priest in retrieving his bags and gathered his own. They walked together toward baggage pickup and as they walked Vernon thanked the man for his council and promised to apply it to his life.

Monday was filled with meetings. Anita Perkins, district manager of North Florida sat beside him during the morning session, but Vernon took a seat between two men down front for the afternoon session. On Tuesday he also arranged to sit away from her. She said nothing but at lunch as he was leaving the buffet line he came face-to-face with her. Her smile told him she understood.

That evening after the meeting Vernon intended to order room service. But his thoughts of Anita took him out of his room and down the lobby of the hotel. He passed the bar and saw Anita seated at a table facing the door.

"Come in. I'm not going to bite you," she said.

"I'm not worried about a bite," he said.

Vernon had often compared Marie and Anita. Marie who kept her hair jet black and wore enough makeup to actually change her appearance and Anita who seemed a natural blonde and wore hardly any makeup. Both beautiful, but so different. Marie, artificial, yet pure. And Anita, natural and worldly. Marie who did things for him. Anita who took as much as she gave.

"Aren't you having a drink?" she asked.

"You know I'm not."

"Look, Vern. You're a big boy. You know the score. And you know my room number. Let's leave it at that. You call me when you want to. I'm not going anywhere." She stood, kissed him on the cheek and left him simmering in the scent of her perfume.

Vernon closed himself in his room and got ready for bed. An early sleep would be just the thing to take him through the next day's meeting and his trip home. He was about to turn the television off when a documentary on the policies of big drug companies caught his attention. He sat propped against the back of the bed talking back to the television.

"Drugs save lives," he shouted at the woman who complained about the high price of medication. "It costs a lot of money to develop a new drug."

During a commercial when he closed his eyes to rest them, images of Marie came to his mind. The morning of his departure she had prepared a big breakfast for him When he finished Marie had taken his hand and led him back to the bedroom. This is where they always said their good-byes. As usual he had left her in bed where she called after him as he walked into the hallway, "Now you be a good boy. I'll be right here waiting for you."

He giggled and mimicked a child. "Okay, Mommy," he said.

Marie always sent him away satisfied and he accepted this as a gift of love. But now and for the first time he had concerns about her motivation. Never look a gift horse . . . but what about dignity. He suddenly had empathy for the drug addict who shows up at the methadone clinic every day when all his being is screaming for the harder stuff.

Music announcing the evening news brought him out of his trance. He felt foolish. What he and Marie had was irreplaceable.

Quickly, he dialed his home number. Marie answered, sleep in her voice. And as they had done since the ultimatum, they talked the talk of those newly in love—sweet words with little substance, spoken by both in a whisper as if they were lying next to each other preparing for the ultimate closeness.

Vernon heard the forty-two before he realized it was the lottery numbers were being announced." Eighteen."

"Hold on, Honey. Just a minute, Honey," he said as he threw the phone on the bed and leaped across to his jacket hanging on the bathroom doorknob.

"Seven."

Vernon trembled as he moved closer to the television.

"Twenty-two."

He began to pace. "Oh, my God," he shouted.

"One."

Vernon removed his T-shirt and whirled it in circles above his head. He saw his reflection as he passed the dresser mirror. Who is this maniac?

"And the super ball number is . . ."

Eight hundred miles away Marie held the phone close to her ear. Sounds of panic and terror came across the line. Sounds of a street gang invasion or a massacre or a sudden tornado. But maybe sounds more like those produced by Vernon on witnessing a winning touchdown.

"Honey, hold on now. Listen. I . . . I mean we . . . they just read . . . we won . . . we won it all. The whole shebang. Eighty seven million dollars. Honey are you there?"

After a few seconds of silence she said, "Oh, Vernon, you've gambled. Do I mean that little to you? I just can't believe . . . ."

"What do you want me to do?" he asked. He plopped down on the bed as if coming to the bench after missing the winning free throw.

"I want you to burn that vile piece of paper and come home to your family, like you were when you left—no more no less."

"Marie, I need to think. I'll call you tomorrow."

"Vernon . . ."

"Good night, Marie."

Calmly, Vernon placed the phone on the bedside table and began to straighten the mess he had made during his victory dance. He put his T-shirt back on and climbed into bed. Lying in the darkness he considered his options.

After about half an hour Vernon jumped from the bed and reached for the phone. He dialed Anita's room.

"Anita, something awful has happened."

"Do you need to talk about it?"

"Oh, yes."

"My door will be open."

She hung up and left Vernon standing with the phone to his ear as if waiting for her to say more. He quickly dressed and was standing in the hall about to close his door when he heard his phone ringing. He closed the door gently—not to disturb the ringing telephone—turned, and walked slowly toward the elevator.

Love in City

Love on a green hillside comes easy.
It has allies:
numerous shades of color,
hundreds of chirps and murmurs,
soft breezes carrying
a multitude of scents
and cooling the spirit.

Love by the sea
has its friends
the rush and return of the waters
bringing earthy sensual smells.
Even in a darkened room
Love by the sea comes easy.

But Love in the city
comes harder.
Among sirens announcing
disaster, injury, Death.
And colors diminished
by the residue of industry
And the smells
of urban flocking.

Yet Love comes.
In an apartment bedroom
with only the wee red light
and the wee blue light
on the stereo to support the scene.
And only music created in a distant studio
to lure the mind to faraway places.
Love comes.

Love and Nature
are complimentary, synergistic,
fodder for the poet.
Love in the city comes out of spite
just to show it can.
It overcomes, survives, triumphs.

Dealing with Slight Hope
1999

It was her way: running wild, flying high, and falling hard. She cleaned up good, as they say, and could stop the crowd when entering a nightspot—hair and nails courtesy of Margie's, outfit carefully chosen from Marshalls or T.J. Maxx, and an air of confidence that she herself supplied.

But deep within her soul the gremlins of self-doubt and self-hate danced to music not unlike rolling thunder. Mornings after were devastating. She wondered how she could produce superfluous tears while her mouth ached with Sahara dryness. What-if became more than just a question for her to ponder. It became an inquisition. She considered self-mutilation in a physical way and practiced it psychologically.

Last night at the Do Drop Inn, she was Aphrodite. Jim Tolerson said so, except he pronounced it Aphroditty. Halvin Montgomery asked her to be his bride. Wendell Wilkerson was more direct and asked her to go to the car with him where he would take her to heights of ecstasy she had only dreamed of. She went with him and found that he had oversold himself by at least eighty percent. If not for the vodka and beer and wine she would have entered a state of gloom right there in the car as he pulled back from her leaving her physically and emotionally empty. But she forged ahead and laughed and shouted and clapped her way through the rest of the evening.

In the morning she awoke with Clark Burt—mouth open, smelling like sour alcohol and stale tobacco—lying beside her. God he was ugly. His comb-over had been dismantled by the night's activity leaving sparse, greasy strands falling over his left ear. And his mechanic's fingernails were black with oil and grease. How could she have let him touch her?

"Clark, time to get up and go, baby."

"Huh?"

"You got to go. I got things to do. Get your ass up."

"Huh?"

She pulled back and gave him a goal kick so hard he was sent flying off the bed and onto her painted concrete floor. His scrawny body hit with a thud.

"What you trying to do, Darleen? Break my neck? Good God."

"Oh, honey, I'm sorry. I guess I don't know my own strength."

He stood before her with no regard to modesty. She turned her eyes wondering how anything that ugly could have lured her into bed.

"Please get dressed and get a move on. Fix yourself a cup of instant to go if you want to."

"Want to take a shower with me?"

"Sounds wonderful, but like I said I got to get moving. Got things to do. Can't you wait till you get home to shower?"

"Yeah, I guess I can. You sure were into me last night. What's changed?"

"Clark, you ought to know by now how I am. Please just go."

He left and Darleen began the degradation process. She started with a review of last night and traveled back and forth through her childhood and teen years and early woman-hood. A wave of nausea swept over her. She did not fight it, but went immediately to the john and spewed the inequities of last night into the bowl. She heaved and gagged trying to remove the last vestige of her sins. The hard floor accepted her and soothed her with its coolness.

When she woke it was near noon. She managed to get to the shower and entered the icy water of castigation. Warmth and comfort were not options. As she dried herself she caught a glimpse of her body in the mirror. She quickly looked away, afraid of seeing snakes for hair, eyes green and bloody, and leper's skin. Anything else would have to be an illusion and she didn't want that—another psychosis.

She dressed slowly. First her oldest undergarments, then the clothes she had worn last week when she painted her room. She lay across the bed, sideways, her wet hair nearly reaching the floor. Tears, moans, gurgles, twists and turns, curses.

The buzz of the doorbell was like the blast from a foghorn. She jumped to her feet and stumbled to the door. Through the peephole she saw old lady Schwartz waiting for her to answer. The old woman moved to and fro showing impatience. Darleen had no choice. She knew the crone had seen her car in the drive. She removed the chain and opened the door.

"Well, hello, Ms. Schwartz. What can I do for you?"

"You can pay your damn rent. That's what you can do. I ought to charge you double for visitors. I seen that skinny Icabod leaving this morning. If you ain't something else."

"I'm sorry. I asked him to come over and fix my television. The cable went out and the cable people said it wasn't their fault."

"Uh huh. That's pretty good. Did it take him all night to fix it? I ain't stupid you know. Well anyway, you can do what you want as long as you don't keep me awake and you pay your damn rent."

"Can I . . . ?"

Darleen stood silent for several seconds trying to come up with the right words and the old landlady mimicked her silence, using only facial expressions to show her impatience.

"Can I have till Wednesday? I get paid on Wednesday."

"Well, what kind of choice do I have? But this is the last time. I know I've told you before, but this time I mean it. You can start looking if you ever come up late again."

The expression on the old lady's face changed from anger to concern. "You need a better job, girl. You ain't never going to amount to nothing selling tickets at the Harper picture show. Hear me?"

"Yes'm. I understand."

Ms. Swartz left as abruptly as she came and as Darleen went back to her bed, she thought, "What's the use. Why do I even bother?" She reached for her cigarettes and found an empty wrapper.

"Clark, you son of a bitch. Damn you."

The trip to Handy Pantry was torture. Her head pounded and her stomach was filled with crawling insects. She nearly hit a Fed Ex truck and took several attempts to parallel park in front of the store. She almost turned around at the entrance to begin her painful journey back to her bed.

But a kind voice and a firm hand on her arm stopped her.

"Darleen?"

She couldn't believe it. Her high school sweetheart stood before her; tall, still handsome and dressed like a GQ model.

"Jimmy Barksdale, is that you? I thought you were in Raleigh."

"It was Durham, but I'm back now. How have you been?"

"Not good. I think I'm going to hell. Figuratively and literally."

"I doubt that. I've often thought of you. About when we went together in high school."

"I'm not that same girl. A lot's happened to me since then. A lot of real bad stuff."

"Maybe we can have coffee and talk."

"I don't think so. You see I don't hang out with people like you."

"Wha . . . ?"

"I don't mean that in a bad way, but a good way. I'd just bring you down."

"Do you think I'm that weak?"

"No, but I think that I'm that rotten."

"Good gosh, Darleen, you are in bad shape."

"You don't know the half of it and I don't want you to. Let's just say goodbye now. I will feel much better if we do."

Darleen turned to go but Jimmy's soft voice held her attention. "Okay. But if you change your mind, you can reach me at the courthouse most days."

"What are you, some kind of judge?"

"Assistant D.A."

"Holy crap. The law."

"I guess. Well, call me sometime."

"I won't, but thanks anyway."

She pushed her way into the store, bought her cigarettes, and started home. She noticed, halfway home, her headache had subsided and her stomach was at ease. Could this unexpected encounter with Jimmy give her relief, relief so sudden and complete? Maybe she should call him.

When she was in high school she was a different person, a better person. But, Jimmy went off to college and things started to sink for her. She tried to remember the exact moment she drifted downward. Impossible. The change was too subtle, a drink here, a promiscuity there. Bottom line: she was never going to be good again. No need to think about Jimmy Barksdale. It would never happen.

But that night she did not go out. And she did think of Jimmy Barksdale. They were parked in Jimmy's Mustang at Hugh Dangerfield State Park. Watching the submarine races. It was the night before Jimmy left for school in North Carolina. She wanted desperately to please him. As always, he started slowly and built up to the point when they both usually stopped, panting and laughing, proud of their restraint. But this night Jimmy did not stop. He said he couldn't. He pleaded for more.

Doreen could hear herself saying, "Baby let's don't. We've waited this long. We have our whole life ahead of us. You understand don't you?" He slowly pulled back and kissed her gently on the cheek. When he left her at her door he gave her a passionate goodbye kiss, their last kiss, and walked hurriedly to his car.

Later that summer with Biff Miller, Jimmy's best friend, at the same lake, in another Mustang, she did not stop. She allowed him to take her that night and every night he chose to be with her.

Now, as she lay in her bed, she realized she had not loved Biff, really had no strong feelings for him. But she had loved Jimmy, adored him. How could she hold back from the one she loved so much and give in so easily to his best friend?

Biff was less than discrete. In fact, he boasted to all the guys that she was a good piece and he could get it any time he wanted. Of course, word got back to Jimmy. And Jimmy never saw her again until this day at the Handy Pantry. He did not call or write. And Darleen in her state of guilt and confusion made no attempt to contact him.

All these thoughts prevented sleep. She got up and down from her bed numerous times during the night, walking to and from the bathroom where she splashed cold water on her face. She puffed away half the cigarettes filling the room with gloomy smoke.

Around three a.m. she approached hysteria. She got out of bed and went out on the front porch of Ms. Schwartz' house. The unoiled springs on the swing sang out a doleful tune as she tried to comfort herself with its back and forth motion. Could she change? Could she ever consider herself worthy? One thing for sure this madness had to stop. But transformations like this don't just happen. It's too simple. Meeting an old boyfriend on the way to buy cigarettes can't be enough to turn a life around.

The moon began to appear just over the hedge in front of the house. It was full and enormous as it climbed into view. She had always thought of the moon as a metaphor for hope. And there it was before her. She felt she could reach out and touch it. But, she knew that no matter how much she stretched, it was beyond her grasp. Just like the slight hope that hovered over her. Frustrating hope, damnable hope.

Then it came to her. The moon is just a hard cold rock. Its purpose is to reflect the rays of the sun. Nothing more. Maybe she had always tried too hard, searching for a quick fix when little steps were called for.

As she walked back to her room she felt a warmth she had not experienced in many years. She sat at her dressing table and looked over dozens of bottles and tubes—nail polish and lipstick—that she used to transform herself into a night creature. The colors were dark and carried names with words like passion, desire, and sin. Her first thought was to sweep all the bottles into a trash-bag. A clean break from the past. But she had tried things like this before. Instead she took a cotton ball and drenched it in nail polish remover. The smell of acetone mingled with the smoke of her cigarette. Small steps. Doreen removed the black polish from the thumb of her left hand and studied the accomplishment. Small steps. The discarded cotton balls, oily and black, accumulated in her trashcan until they nearly reached the top.

When she had cleaned each nail on her hands and feet, she stretched her arms and legs out toward the light from the rising sun, to make sure she had removed all the blackness. A single ray of sun slipped past the edge of the window shade and settled on the top of the waste can. It its brightness the cotton balls looked bright and clean. She could see no darkness, for this moment no darkness at all.

LURES
2002

Around Harper when people think about or talk about lures it's about the kind that are attached to the end of your line to attract and hook a fish. Not Merijoan Fitzbanks. She thinks of New Orleans, the French Quarter, loose women, and the story of her two lost sons.

The Fitzbanks run a house painting company. In fact, their house, the first and only duplex in Harper serves not only as their home and office, but also as an advertisement for their business. They keep one side painted and let the other stand and weather. In the yard they have placed two signs. In front of the unpainted side: BEFORE and the attended side: AFTER. Old man Fitzbanks died back in the 90's and Merijoan and her three boys took over the business and did real well as far as we could tell. Everything was percolating the way Merijoan would have wanted it. That is until Billy Joe, her youngest boy went to New Orleans with a group of his friends.

He did not come home.

When his friends were questioned they told a tale of Billy Joe and a woman who called herself Tanya Hyde all tangled in a romantic affair. Billy was a good-looking fellow and was always considered a good catch for the local girls.

In an act of desperation Merijoan sent her middle son, Karl Buck, down to New Orleans to fetch her youngest son and bring him back to all the pleasantries and comfort of home. Karl Buck didn't come back either.

For two weeks we all held our breath, watched, and waited for the two lost boys to return. That was long enough for Merijoan. She didn't jump into action, however she did begin to formulate a rescue plan. Her first step was to seek the council of Reverent Bubba Blatt, her preacher. She requested his prayers and advice. He thought the situation over and suggested she appoint

Bartholomew, her oldest boy, ambassador with the duty of rescuing his brothers. Bartholomew was married and considerably more stable than his younger brothers.

Merijoan shook her head. "Can't do it," she said. "I need that boy to run the business. We couldn't afford to lose him too."

"Then I'll go," said Reverent Bubba.

"No, no, no," said Merijoan. "We can't afford to lose you neither."

That night Merijoan sat down and put her plan of action down on paper. She developed a list of all the things she could think of:

1. What is the penalty for battery in the state of Louisiana?
2. Which lawyer would be most likely to keep me out of jail?
3. Weapon?
4. Clothes best to wear when swinging a baseball bat at a slut.
5. How much . . . .

At number five her mind shifted to another list, things to pack for the trip to New Orleans. She could think of only two entries for this list:

1. Baseball bat.
2. Holy Bible.

The Bible lay beside her bed, easy to access for nightly study. The baseball bat was stored in her bedroom closet behind a stack of shoeboxes. It had been removed from her car years ago when the preacher called her into his office and warned her of the wrath of the Lord and, not to be minimized, the wrath of the State if she carried out the treat she had publically issued against Maywinnie Baltz, a local hairdresser. Maywinnie had been spotted parked out at Harper Lake in a car in the moonlight with Merijoan's husband.

So off she went to the city wearing a red dress, hopeful it would not show blood and announce her deed. In the passenger seat lay the bat and the Bible. She adjusted the rear view mirror to check her hair and saw killing in her eyes. She felt an urge in her heart to rid the world of all loose women.

The highway down to New Orleans runs through a stretch of swampland. There is something about watching mile after mile of gnarled leafless trees stretching out of murky brown water that makes a person think. A lot of minds have changed direction going through this territory. It gives hope in a way because you know it's not going to last forever. Solid ground lies ahead.

Merijoan experienced an epiphany about twenty miles into the swamplands just as the sun was rising. When she left Harper she fully intended to put all her stock into swinging that baseball bat. But as she looked out over the water she was caught in the grasp of a bright streak of sunlight. It summoned her to pray. And during that prayer her mission changed from murder to missionary work. She determined to convert these sinful women. They would become lures for the Lord.

Merijoan pulled off of I-10 and entered the French Quarter around 9 AM. It had been years since she had driven in New Orleans and the only thing that kept her from pulling over and breaking down was a gritty determination to complete her mission. After circling the block where she had been given the address of her youngest son's whereabouts she spotted a vacant parking space. Vacant except for a one foot pile of spent oyster shells. She accomplished a somewhat straight position in the spot after several back and forths over the pile of shells.

The stairway up to the second floor apartment was dark and needed painting. She thought a nice gray would work nicely. The number 13 was painted in bright yellow over the royal blue peeling paint of the door. Merijoan knocked.

After about ten minutes of banging the door opened as far as the security chain would allow and Merijoan was greeted with a pair of Maybelline eyes.

"Yes?"

"I'm Billy Joe's mamma and I got something for y'all," said Merijoan.

"Come on in," said Tanya.

This is what Merijoan told the ladies of the Ladies Christian Club at her church:

"There she stood, this harlot looking creature in a skimpy night gown with the top part of her body kinda leaking out. Her hair was big and looked like it had been through a thunderstorm. All her nails were painted black and some of her makeup had wore off on one side. I reckon she left it on her pillow. I have to tell y'all she was a shapely little thing and I could see where a good hot bath and a trip to my beauty parlor could make her into Harper material."

Merijoan looked around the cluttered apartment. She was astonished to see empty beer bottles and fast food wrappers everywhere.

"This place is a mess," she said.

Tanya didn't say anything. She just backed up a step.

Merijoan opened her Bible and began to read from passages she had bookmarked with business cards from her painting business.

Tanya looked as if she was being confronted by a terrorist or a rapist. She backed up again until the wall with the wide screen TV stopped her.

When Merijoan finished her prepared sermon she said, "I got me a room at a bed and breakfast just down the street and I plan to come back every day until you see the light. And that's a promise."

Tanya said she would not have it. She said she would get Billy Joe to stop his mother's harassment.

"Well honey, you can try. But I better warn you them boy's really love their mamma."

That night when Billy Joe came home from his job at Deal Mart, Tanya told him of his mother's threat. But not until they were climbing into bed. She had on her most seductive bedclothes and was wearing a perfume called Wildness. As she talked, almost sung, her plea for rescue, Billy Joe sat beside her. He drew imaginary pictures on the carpet with his big toe and looked up at the ceiling as if the answer to this dilemma was painted there.

After a minute or two Billy Joe said, "Tanya, you know how much I told you I love you? Well I do. But when it comes down to making you mad or making mamma mad I'll side with my mamma every time."

"I just don't understand how you come to live with me, sleep with me every night, and pick that old woman's side of the argument. Why did you leave her in the first place?"

"I reckon it's a distance thing, honey. When she was a hundred miles away her pull was on me was not so great. But, Good Lord, she's sleeping only a block away as we speak."

The next morning Merijoan showed up just as she promised, opened her Bible, and started in on sermon number two.

That's when Tanya was forced to play her ace in the hole, a card even Billy Joe didn't know about.

"Lady, you need to know I am carrying your grandbaby."

One of Merijoan's strongest beliefs was that a marriage that wasn't performed in a church wasn't a marriage at all. But sometimes when faced with a real hard decision a person will often take a path that doesn't completely consider all their principles. Merijoan had spotted a little wedding chapel right down the street from where she was staying. In fact she could see the entrance from her room at the bed and breakfast and had spent many minutes shaking her head in utter disdain for those who entered and left this establishment. She arranged a wedding ceremony as quickly as the state would allow it. Tanya was delighted and Billy Joe seemed happy enough. Merijoan was content just to free her son from living in sin.

Packing didn't take long with Merijoan in charge and within a week of her arrival in New Orleans Merijoan, her son Billy Joe, and her new daughter-in-law, now a student in the ways of good clean living, were headed back across the swamps and on their way to their home in Harper.

Marijoan spent the next week installing her boy and his bride in their new home, a two bedroom cottage on the lake side of her property. The little house had one been occupied by her brother, a World War II veteran who had never married and finally succumbed to the wounds of battle and the collapse of his cigarette lungs. Merijoan told the church lady group that while she was blessed by her brother's presence on earth the Lord knew when a person's burden was too hard and had relieved her of the responsibility of taking care of his needs.

Once Billy Joe and Tanya were moved in and settled, Merijoan got back in her car and headed to the French Quarter. This time she was lifted by the success of her first rescue and left her baseball bat at home. She did expect a different, a better outcome with this trip. If her boy had enough sense not to put his woman in a family way she would use all her energy in running her off in order to bring her son back alone. Then she would work on marrying him off to a good Harper girl.

When she arrived she had a déjà vu moment. The stairway looked the same and there was the same number 13 painted on the door except this time the number was red and the door was green. Of a sudden Merijoan sensed the worse and sure enough the woman who opened the door was showing a pregnancy that Merijoan guessed to be about four months in progress. Carl Buck must have rung that one up on his first week or something else had been going on.

Since Merijoan was familiar with all the rules for getting a boy married in the state of Louisiana this time things were easier and quicker. A few days later the trio headed back to Harper with Merijoan driving and Carl Buck and Mayjean, that was his new wife's name sitting in the backseat. She had to tell them several time to cut out their romancing.

"Just 'cause y'all married don't mean you can start face sucking anytime you want to. Wait till you get back in your room and you can do what ever you want. As long as I don't have to hear it."

Carl Buck and Mayjean moved into the house with his mother until she could find a better accommodation for them. This process was speeded up when Merijoan either heard or thought she heard what she referred to as tribal grunts coming from the upstairs room. Luckily the little house right next door that Merijoan rented out to a insurance salesman came vacant when she informed him of a substantial rent increase and told him he could no longer smoke on her property.

Now that she had both sons home, married and living close by she decided on building a sidewalk between the two houses so the girls could easily get together. In her way of thinking this would help them adapt a little better to small town life.

Tanya was a better recruit than Mayjean. She accepted advice and tried to follow the directives of her mother in law. All this indoctrination did not set well with the other daughter in law. She had a yearning look in her eye and Marijoan knew in her heart the marriage of her middle son was doomed. She once over heard a conversation between Tanya and Mayjean.

"How come you let that old woman boss you around like that. She's got you cutting back on your makeup, cooking what she wants you to cook, and going to that holy rolly church she goes to. How can you stand to be around her."

"Well," replied Tanya. "She's the closest thing to a mother I ever had."

Mayjean didn't make it through the winter. This man, a cowboy looking fellow, was down at the Do Drop Inn one night when Mayjean stopped in for a little refreshment on her way back from the grocery store and it didn't take her an hour to secure a place in his car for a trip out of town. She didn't even leave a note or anything for Carl Buck. He didn't seem to be too upset about it and Merijoan felt things had worked out just fine.

At one of her church meeting one of the women got up the nerve to ask Merijoan about her runaway daughter in law.

"Well, I can't say anything bad about her. But I'll bet she can describe in fine detail the ceiling of several French Quarter bedrooms."

Tanya and Billy Joe are doing well. Most people in Harper have accepted her as one who has seen the evil of their ways and is trying to be a good person. A few have not. But they are the same once who believe dancing is a sin and are strongly against premarital sex for fear it may lead to dancing.

Carl Buck is going with a sweet little woman from the church. She is meek and kind and seems to have his best interest at heart. Merijoan has told him if he plays his cards right he can bring her home as his bride and she will foot the bill for the wedding dress as long as it isn't a maternity/wedding dress.

Merijoan now live alone. Her Bible is on the table by her bed. The baseball bat was stuffed back in the closet until recently. After many hours of thoughtful meditation it was decided to display it above the living room mantel, a symbol of restraint and wisdom during struggling times.

May Margaret's Christmas Extravaganza 2009

May Margaret stood in a kitchen filled with flour fog. The table and counter tops were covered with a whiteness not unlike the hoar frost that had covered the field earlier in the morning. Clutter was a symptom of her cooking habits making cleanup the most time consuming part of the job. She moved to the window and peered out at the her sister's ten year old Cadillac pulling into the yard

Esther Agnes was always first to arrive. Somebody had to look out for the noodle-heads. It was the ninth annual visit to May Margaret's house for Christmas Eve celebration. Esther Agnes lived in a much finer house. It was too nice for this crowd. When their mother Grandma Florabelle's house received extensive damage from a fire one April evening—a blaze started when a parched Christmas tree, still lighted nightly, exploded—the event needed a new home. Esther Agnes was not in the running. She was reluctant to have even the Women's Missionary Union over, for fear one of the less worthy members would spill Kool-Aid on one of her fine chairs. Her family coming to her house was out of the question.

As she drove up the gravel driveway, she slowed and looked around as if something was wrong. The yellow bus with Harper County Schools in black print along its sides was parked beside the house, where it should be. Brightly lit icicles hung from the eaves of the house and were draped over three dead automobiles rusting in the front yard. But they had been there since Cleveron hung them five years ago. No, something else was different. Missing. It was the dogs. Usually when Esther Agnes pulled up the drive she was greeted by ten or twelve barking canines all colors, shapes, and sizes. Tonight there was silence.

Esther Agnes, a tall Olive Oyle type, had to bend to avoid the hanging icicles. She wore a holiday pantsuit with a thousand sequins.

"Yoo-hoo, May Margaret, I'm here. I brought the rice and gravy and the lime Jell-O with celery and bananas that I do."

"Well, come on in, sister, and take a load off," said May Margaret. "Here let me take some of that. I'll put your Jell-O in the icebox."

May Margaret was a wide, multi-chinned woman with orange hair and orange lipstick. She wore a cherry red sweat suit. Her sneakers were pink.

"Where's them dogs? They weren't there to knock me down and tear up my panty hose like they did last year."

"Somebody borrowed them. Just for one night. They gonna play parts in a Christmas pageant over at that new church up there close to the county line. You know the one that used to be a house and now it's a church? Some are gonna be cows and some are gonna be sheep. And Sparky is gonna be one of the wise men. They're one wise man short, being a new church and all. They could be a shepherd short and nobody would even notice, but you just got to have three wise men. And Sparky's big and can walk a short distance on his hind legs, so . . ."

"Well I never heard such foolishness. Dogs in the church. God ain't going like that."

"I thought of that. No, they ain't going to take them dogs in the church. It's all outside. I made sure of that." Esther Agnes paused in front of the Christmas tree.

"Don't you think that Christmas tree is a little big? It's bent over a foot at the top across the ceiling."

"Well, I do. I agree," said May Margaret. "But Cleveron won't cut top or bottom. He says it'd mess up the shape if we went to slicin' on it. I couldn't put up that big star that Mamma give us. It's got me worrying about hurtin' her feelings. You know how touchy she is especially around the holidays. Listen, here comes Harvey Lynn and Betty Fay. Wish he'd break down and get that muffler fixed. Every year you can hear them before they get to the Rumble Road turnoff."

"How many kids they got now? Is it seven or eight?"

"Nope. It ain't but five, just seems like more. Them's the baddest kids in town. Well not bad, just mis-chee-vee-ous. They always into something. I believe that if my first children were twins I would have taken it as a sign to stop right there."

Harvey Lynn, their younger brother, stomped up the steps. He was followed by twin boys both wearing Peyton Manning jerseys and New

Orleans Saints caps. Next came two girls one ten and the other nine. The girls' hair hung in a loose array of woven loops. They wore sweaters, jeans and flip-flops. A barefoot three year old, wearing a heavy sweater over a diaper, broke free from her mother's grasp and headed for the steps.

"You kids get in here and shut your traps. If I have to take my belt off y'all going to be sorry as a shot rabbit." Harvey was good at simile. "Lynwood, you and Elwood bring in them presents. Florene, you and Irene bring in them pies and don't drop none. Maxine, come on in honey. You want Daddy-pop to help you up the steps?"

"No, Daddy-pop, I three and a half. I do it all by . . ." The little girl lay spread eagle tripped by a root. She got up crying.

"Here, let Daddy-pop dust you off. You okay? Betty Faye, come see about your daughter. And wipe off her nasty nose."

Betty crab-walked up the steps. She was in the eighth month of her fifth pregnancy and was exceedingly large. It was obvious that it was time for her weekly shampoo.

"I reckon we better let them in," May Margaret said to Esther Agnes as they watched from the picture window of the living room.

"That girl's big as a barn," said Esther Agnes. "She get any bigger she gonna pop."

May Margaret held the door open and stepped back out of the way of the rush of children.

"Y'all get yourself in this house," she said.

"Whoa," said Elwood. "That's a damn big tree."

With what appeared to be a familiar swiftness, Harvey Lynn unbuckled his belt, released it from its loops, and delivered a pop to the left buttock of his first-born child.

"What'd I do? What'd I do," screamed the twelve-year-old.

His brother, younger by mere minutes, whooped out a laugh.

Harvey Lynn swung the belt in his direction and hit his left buttock in a spot almost identical to the area where his brother was struck.

"Don't you be laughin' at the misfortune of others. Now I done warned you boys I ain't goin' to put up with no foolishness. Y'all go out in the yard and let go of some of your energy before grandma gets here. She don't need to be dealin' with no dumb boys in her condition and all."

"What about me?" said Esther Agnes. "I got high blood. I don't need no dumb boys actin' up around me neither."

The boys went into the yard and began to hit at the icicles with sticks.

A fifteen-year-old Cadillac pulled into the drive and parked as close to the front door as possible. The driver, Clara Susan, the younger sister of May Margaret and Ester Agnes, got out and walked around to the passenger side. Clara was a pretty girl in her mid-twenties. She wore a gray skirt, white blouse, and a blue blazer with a gold patch on the pocket. In her left hand he carried a copy of *The English Patient*.

Her mother, Florabelle Swinston, waited until Clara had opened the door. Then she began a moanful exit from the car.

"Be patient, Clara Susan. I ain't as young as I used to be. Oh. Oh. Oh. Not so fast, damn it. My leg. And my back."

"Sorry, Mother. I'm trying to move along with you. At your speed."

"Well you ain't doin' too good. Are you?"

After a five-minute struggle, the mother and daughter stood on the porch and waited for the door to open for them.

"Ring the bell," said Florabelle as she adjusted the synthetic fabric of her sky blue pants. "These damn things creep up on me every time I get in that car."

"The bell hasn't worked for years."

"Then knock. I'm gonna catch the flooze standing out here in the dark."

"It's seventy-five degrees. You're not going to catch the flu."

"And who are you to predict the future? Just because you went to college. You didn't even study to make a doctor or nothin'. You just learned to read books."

May Margaret opened the door and stepped onto the porch and took her mother's arm. Clara Susan returned to the car and retrieved an aluminum walker and a portable oxygen tank. She took them to her mother.

May Margaret spoke, "Here, let me help you, Mamma. Is that a new wig you wearin'?"

"Nope, just got it out of moth balls. I wanted a red one for Christmas."

"Well it sets you off right admirable, Mamma. You go on in, Clara Susan. What you readin' this time?"

"The English Patient."

"What makes them so patient? They weren't so patient with George Washington and all the columnists. Were they?"

"No they weren't," said Clara Susan. "Not at all."

Clara Susan had long since given up on explanations.

Once inside, Florabelle stood before the tree with her mouth open. "That's the biggest damn tree I ever saw," she said.

May Margaret and Esther Agnes rushed around in the kitchen finishing up the preparation of the Christmas feast. It took both of them to lift the turkey from the oven and set it up on top of the stove. May Margaret scooped the regular dressing and the oyster dressing into matching bowls. She placed the plastic oyster shell that she kept for this occasion, on top of the one with oysters. Esther Agnes dished out ambrosia into little pudding cups. She made sure each one had half a maraschino cherry on top. They set the main table for the adults and pushed a couple of card tables together for the children.

"Don't forget my rice and gravy and lime Jell-O," said Esther Agnes.

"Wouldn't forget that, sister," said May Margaret. "Clara Susan, put that book down and get in here and help your old sisters."

"I didn't want to get in the way," said Clara Susan.

"Well you could put some ice in these glasses and pour in the sweet tea. Don't you reckon everybody wants sweet tea, Esther Agnes?" said May Margaret.

"Why wouldn't they?" said Esther Agnes.

The barking of a dozen dogs could be heard from the yard.

"They's here. They's here," said May Margaret. "We can eat now. Oh, happy day."

Cleveron could be heard stomping the mud off his boots on the front steps. He entered the house and nodded a greeting to his guests. He was six foot four when he stood up straight, which he rarely did. He wore a St. Louis Cardinal baseball cap and his denim shirt was unbuttoned revealing a Budweiser T-shirt.

"Well, don't you have nothin' to say?" asked Florabelle.

"Hello, Mamma."

"He speaks," said Mamma.

"Let's all sit down. Y'all sit where you want to. Esther Agnes you sit here. Clara Susan, you and Mamma sit on this side, and Harvey Lynn and Betty Faye, you sit next to Esther Agnes. Cleveron and me will sit at each end. Now ain't this cozy."

"I guess I'll return thanks," said May Margaret. "Y'all all bow your heads and close your eyes. Dear Lord, bless this food to the nourishment of our bodies. And help us as we go through this life to make the right decisions. Bless Esther Agnes as she tries to get over her husband running off with that piano player from the church all those years ago. She needs to be strong. And if it be thy will, render unto that man all the punishment that you see fit. And that piano playing woman, too. And please help Clara Susan to get interested in a man. We all worry so much about her and her situation. They's so many good men around here. If I sat down and thought, I could name five or six that would be good for her. And bless Mamma. Help her as she goes through her search for teeth that fit. It must be awful to have a mouth full of teeth that don't fit. Bless Harvey Lynn and Betty Faye as they expand their family. Give them the wisdom to know when to quit. And bless them kids of theirs. Teach them to be quiet and respectful and to help their mamma and daddy with the new baby coming and all. And help them twin boys with their boils. Teach them not to pick at them so they can get well. And, Dear Lord, bless Cleveron. Help him to get back on at the panty factory. And help all the others who got let go. It don't seem right. Ladies got to have panties even if times are bad. Thank God I still got my school bus job. We pray a special blessing on our boy in San Francisco. Keep him safe from all that goes on there. The things we see on Fox News and all. And help our boy in New Orleans workin' in that nightclub. I know he can sing good, but he could be singing church songs. And bless his roommate. It still don't seem right living in the same apartment with a member of the opposite sex, but so many things don't seem right. And help our new president. It must be real hard on him tryin' to run a country. It would be hard even for a white man, so please be with him and guide him. I reckon since he's been elected we all need for him to do good. We ask all these blessings in Christ's name. Amen."

"Amen," said the group.

"And God bless us everyone," said Clara Susan.

"Pass to the left, please," said May Margaret. "Cleveron, slice up some turkey. Y'all pass your plates down and tell him what you want, white meat or dark meat. We got both."

"Now y'all be sure and try my rice and gravy and the lime Jell-O," said Esther Agnes. "I spent a long time cutting up celery and bananas."

"Cleveron, how did the pageant go? Did Sparky behave?" said May Margaret.

"He done okay. He was a cow."

"I thought he was gonna be a wise man."

"No, they wanted me to be a wise man, so I did."

"How ironic," said Clara Susan.

"Yeah, I wore this maroon colored bathrobe and one of them old ladies wrapped a turbine hat on my head and I walked right down with these two other men. I was Gold and one of them was Murray and the other was Frankenstein."

"Lord help us," said Clara Susan.

"Praise the Lord," said May Margaret.

After dessert, May Margaret, Esther Agnes, Harvey Lynn, Betty Faye, and Florabelle produced cigarette packs and laid them on the table. Five smokers, five brands. They lit up with the matches that were part of their place setting.

"Y'all can use your dessert plates for ash trays," said May Margaret.

"Betty Faye, do you think you ought to smoke during your pregnancy?" asked Clara Susan.

"I reckon it's okay. I smoked during all the others and they turned out just fine. Besides mine has a filter on it. Takes out all the bad stuff."

"Well if you don't mind I'll excuse myself and go to the living room to read," said Clara Susan. "See you when we open gifts."

After the smoke-fest the group assembled in the living room in front of the gigantic tree and began to hand out gifts. The kids were first, so they could take their toys and move out of the grown-up's way. Then the group waited until their mother had opened her presents. Florabelle got perfume, an eggbeater with a wooden handle, a blue and green shawl, and a year's subscription to *The Upper Room*.

After the rest had opened and expressed enthusiasm over their Christmas bounty, May Margaret said, "I got a surprise for all of you. A little something extra. Cleveron and me went to Biloxi and we seen these T-shirts that we liked and we picked one out for each of you. Here's yours, Esther Agnes. We know how proud you are of your education so we got this one for you."

Esther Agnes took the shirt and held it in front of her. It said: I WENT ALL THE WAY IN HIGH SCHOOL. "Well all I can say is I love it," she said.

May Margaret handed Clara Susan her shirt. "Yours says: I'M AVAILABLE on the front and we had your cell phone number put on the back. See? 601-555-2222."

"Thank you so much," said Clara Susan. "I'll wear it every time I take a nap."

"Huh? Well any way we hope it does great things for you."

Florabelle's shirt said on the front: IF MAMMA AIN'T HAPPY AIN'T NOBODY HAPPY. And on the back: AND WE AIN'T NEVER HAPPY.

Everyone laughed except Florabelle and Clara Susan.

Harvey Lynn's said: I'M REAL GOOD AT DOING NOTHING.

And Betty Fay's: ANOTHER ONE IN THE OVEN.

"Well, Cleveron just wanted another Budweiser, a red one to go with his blue one. And mine, I don't mind a little self teasing." And she held up: I MAY BE FAT BUT I'M SLOW.

After things slowed down a little, Clara Susan reached in the pocket of her blazer and took out an engagement ring. She slid it on her finger.

"I've got one more present to show you," she said to the group. She held up her hand and watched the shocked look on the faces of her family.

"Well who in the world is he?" said May Margaret.

"A guy I met at LSU. He's from New York."

Florabelle reached for her oxygen mask, put it to her face, and breathed deeply. "A Yankee? Oh my Lord. A damn Yankee."

"Well, that's nice," said Esther Agnes. "Just please don't tell us he's a Catholic."

"He is. He is a very devout Catholic," said Clara Susan.

With that announcement the group fell silent except for muffled sniffles from the four women.

Florabelle disconnected her air supply and stood with the aid of her walker. "I want to go home right now. I need to go to bed and I may never get out of it. That's how much of shock you've brought to me, girl. Selfish, selfish girl."

Cleveron looked confused. "Well at least he ain't no Jew or niggerow."

"Shut up, Cleveron," said May Margaret.

The party broke up quickly as all rushed to their vehicles for the trip home.

After they were gone, May Margaret turned to Cleveron and said, "Well all in all you'd have to say this was another successful Christmas. But tomorrow we better start getting' ready for next year. We have so much to do."

"Well, the lights is up," said Cleveron.

"They's a lot more do to next year. We gonna have a special newcomer and he's from New York and he's a Catholic. I gotta read up on all that stuff. Gotta get some new recipes. I think I heard somewhere that Catholics are supposed to eat fish."

"I sure as hell know how to catch fish," said her husband.

"But I need recipes. Wonder if they have a New York cookbook with catfish recipes. And we need to go to Jackson to the Baptist Book Store and get one of them crosses. I wonder if the Catholics have a book store. Oh, Cleveron, ain't it gonna be great?"

Another Christmas Extravaganza 2010

Tony Pisano watched the Southwest Mississippi landscape as it passed the window of his new Porsche. The last vestige of fall presented itself with brown leaves mottled with an occasional red or yellow spot. Fields with a cow here and there, long chicken houses with tin roofs, and short two-lane bridges over narrow creeks and streams did little to pull his attention away from the fears permeating his brain. Today was the day he would meet Susan's family.

Susan had not balked on coming with him to Brooklyn to attend his Christmas celebration. His family was excited about her visit and had rearranged the holiday festivities to allow the newly weds to honor both families with their presence. Everything had gone well, certainly better than he had expected. He had not worried about his parents; they were steady and adapted well to all kinds of situations. It was the others that caused him concern. His brother Dom, braggadocio and schemer, had often caused a riff between Tony and girls he brought home. Dom was a multi-level marketer and always had a new company with benefits "better than anything I've ever seen." Dom could not resist spreading the word and approached any stranger with a line more enthusiastic than a street missionary.

And his sister, Mary Frances, usually pulled his girls off to the side and wept out the sad story of her latest betrayal by a man. "I just wish I could find one man who kept his asshole well-hidden in his briefs and didn't have it sticking up out of his collar," she had told more than one visitor. Tony had tried to convince her that her lament did not make good sense and she should play around with different verbiage, if it was necessary to say anything at all on this subject. But to no avail, the asshole story was ever present on these social occasions.

Uncle Rudolph thought he could sing. As a young man he had entered Saturday contests at the Bijou, the local movie house. He had never won, but his mother, now being sung to by a chorus of heavenly hosts, never let up on her encouragement and had plastered kudos over any negativity that might have arisen from years of rejection.

It must have been intervention by his parents, for Susan's benefit, because Dom only talked about Eli Manning and the Giants and Mary Frances brought a date, a lanky, ill-dressed young man with scars from bouts of acne during his teen years and an Adam's apple the size of a small tangerine. All during the night Mary Frances clung to this guy whose name turned out to be Benny Gaye. She laughed with an adolescent giggle at everything Benny said and offered complements, profuse and unrealistic, considering the homely appearance and Gump-like comments of her guest. Uncle Rudolph did not attend. He had called early in the day complaining of a gout attack so severe he was unable to wear any shoe. Even his slipper caused him agony he had reported.

So things had gone well and Susan seemed to be delighted at the warmth and light-hearted spirit of a New York Italian Christmas. Would Susan's family's acceptance of him be as warm? He had reason for concern. Susan had joked with him about her family's intolerance toward Yankees and Catholics. All this was funny to her; at least she presented it that way. Tony was terrified of what lay ahead. Especially meeting Susan's mother. The old woman had refused to attend the wedding and was said to have taken to her bed for a week and stayed cooped up in her house for a month before and after the ceremony.

"Turn right. Down this gravel road, honey." Susan moved closer to her husband and placed her hand on his thigh and patted soothingly. This was intended, he was sure, to comfort him, but the effect was the opposite. Just the idea that Susan felt he needed to be consoled heightened his anxiety.

"Remember, they call me Clara Susan, but you still must call me Susan. Maybe it will catch on with them. I doubt it, but maybe. And remember I'll be right beside you. Not a one of them has been educated past high school so keep the subject simple and whatever you do, do not talk about religion or politics. It would be like arguing with retard . . ." Susan stopped herself and he knew she too was nervous because she never used terms considered politically incorrect.

A yellow school bus parked beside an aging ranch style house, lighted icicles, and a pack of mangy dogs told Tony they had arrived. Susan had painted a picture so close to reality it startled him. "Wow! You really nailed the description of May Margaret's house. I hope those dogs don't jump on my car."

"Let me out at the mailbox and I'll walk up and get things under control."

Susan jumped out and yelled out for her brother-in-law. "Cleveron, come help get these dogs under control.

Cleveron came out the front door and stood on the front porch for a few seconds. It was his way to take a little time to assess any situation, no matter how obvious, before making a move. "Sparky, Dank, Honky, Hazel. Y'all get on up her and get in your pen. "Come on, Elvis and Cash. Here, Mizlou. Y'all get your butts on up here."

Tony watched with astonishment as the seven dogs moved into single file formation and marched toward a chicken wire enclosure just visible behind the school bus. "Y'all get on in there and I'll feed you soon."

Tony drove slowly behind Susan as she made her way up to the house. She turned and signaled for him to stop and park behind an old Cadillac and a GMC truck with the biggest wheels he had ever seen.

"Cleveron, this is my husband, Tony. Tony, Cleveron."

Cleveron reached out a paw twice the size of Tony's hand and as rough and calloused as canvas.

"I'm glad you got to meet me," said Cleveron.

"He's glad to meet you," said Susan.

"Likewise."

"Huh?"

"He's glad to meet you too, Cleveron."

"Oh. You from New York ain't you?" said Cleveron. "You ever been up on top of the Umpire Steak Building?"

"The Empire State Building," said Susan.

"Yes, I have."

"Well, gosh doggies," said Cleveron.

"He's impressed," said Susan.

Susan stopped at the door and stood for a few seconds as if to compose herself before making the grand entrance. Then she took Tony's arm and escorted him into the living room. And there before Tony's bewildered eyes a scene—not unlike one from the TV show *Hee Haw*—slowly developed. He knew who they were without introduction: Mama Florabelle, Ethyl Agnes, May Margaret, Harvey Lynn and his wife Betty Faye, and their kids whose names he had made no attempt to learn. Susan went through the formalities anyway and everyone enthusiastically welcomed the new family member with the obvious exception of Mama who snuggled deeper into a once beige recliner and breathed deeply through her oxygen mask.

"Tommy," said Cleveron.

"Tony. His name is Tony," said Susan.

"That's what I said," said Cleveron. "Tony, want to go outside and shoot the shotgun. We can play skeets. I got some of them large Pepsi bottles filled with colored water we can shoot at. They make a pretty sight when you hit one."

"I don't think my accuracy would yield a fun event for you," said Tony.

Cleveron did not respond but stood with his mouth agape.

"He said he's not into guns," said Susan.

"Not into guns? Dog biscuits," said Cleveron.

"He said he understands." Susan took Tony by the hand and let him over to where her mother was sitting.

The old woman pulled a shawl up over her chin and appeared to be contemplating covering her entire head.

"Mama, this is Tony, my husband. Tony, this is Mama."

"Yeah, I figured that out when I saw y'all come in. I didn't think you'd be bringing no man to Christmas that warn't your husband. Besides you said he was a Italian and he sure looks like a Italian."

"Thanks, Mama."

"Nice to meet you, Ms. Florabelle," said Tony.

"Humph," said Mama.

"And this is my sister, Esther Agnes. She lives in that little brick house I pointed out as we were leaving Harper."

"I've never considered it little, but what ever you say, Susan. You're the college graduate."

"Nice to meet you Esther Agnes. And your house is beautiful. I sure didn't think it was little."

"Oh, my,' said Esther Agnes to Susan. "You may have caught a good'n here, girl."

"And this is May Margaret."

"I've heard about your culinary skills," said Tony as he reached for her hand. But May Margaret just stood there, hands to her side.

"He's heard what a good cook your are," said Susan.

"Oh, my goodness," said May Margaret with a giggle. "What a gentleman you have here, Susan."

"Humph," said Mama.

From outside came a loud bang followed by the laughter and screams of children. Tony walked to the door and looked out just as Cleveron tossed a liter Pepsi bottle into the air. He fired and the bottle exploded showering the dirt yard with red colored water. The kids shouted out their approval.

May Margaret reached out and took Tony's arm. I cooked something special just for you. I somehow got the idea you would like fish and I have been looking over cookbooks all year for a New York catfish dish. The best I could come up with was a combination of catfish baked in Manhattan clam chowder. I hope you like it."

"I'm sure I will," said Tony as he suppressed a gag that was gathering in his throat.

"What ya do?," said Betty Faye. "I mean for a living."

"I'm working on my PhD."

"He's still in school," said Susan. "But he's writing a book too."

"Oh, writing a book," said Ethyl Agnes. "What's it about."

"A story about a family in New Orleans during the Great Depression. It's fiction."

"It's a made-up story," said Susan.

"I know what friction is," said Ethyl Agnes.

May Margaret went into the kitchen and a few minutes later came and called them all in for dinner. She went onto the front porch and called Cleveron and told the children to go wash up and sit quietly at the two card tables she had put against the dining room wall for them.

When they were seated May Margaret gave the blessing. She prayed for all the things she usually prayed for but this year she added a special request for Tony. "And please, Lord, help Tony to understand our ways and to accept them, maybe even adopt them, if it be Thy will. Let him see we are good, Christian people who try to always follow the Bible and do Thy will. Let him understand why we don't believe in worshiping statues and why our preachers don't wear robes. Let him see that we can confess direct to Thee and don't need to go through no saints. Let him understand that we think Mother Mary was a wonderful woman and had a special place in Thy plan. But show him how that's all she is and she ain't a part of the Trinity or nothing like that."

"Please say amen," said Susan. "I think Tony has received your message."

"Amen," said May Margaret. "It wasn't no message. It was a blessing. Cleveron, will you start the fish around."

Tony was tentative and took only a tiny bit of fish on his fork. To his astonishment it was delicious. "Boy, this fish is really good," he said and looked May Margaret right in the eye and held his glance until he saw the smile appear on her face.

"She ain't never cooked nothing that warn't," said Mama. "Humph."

Gifts were exchanged. The children tore into theirs and disappeared into parts of the house left unknown to Tony.

"They're usually not this good," Susan whispered to her husband. "I think you have them mesmerized."

"Why?" asked Tony.

"Because you are from New York. All they know about New York is big and enticing: the Yankees, tall buildings, exciting TV shows and movies."

Later, as Susan and Tony were making the return trip, back through Harper and on to McComb and I-55, they revisited their evening at May Margaret's. Susan apologized for the didactic blessing, for Cleveron's ineptitude, and for the numerous arguments that accompanied the gift giving. "I hope things weren't too bad for you," she said.

Tony slowed the Porche and eased it to a stop on the side of the road.

"Why are we stopping?" said Susan.

"Because I have an irresistible urge to kiss my wife," replied Tony.

For a few seconds they just sat and looked ahead. There seemed to be no cars on the road. Maybe everyone in the county was still occupied with Christmas celebrations.

Susan spoke first. "I am so glad all that is over. I was so worried my family would make you want to run for the Mason Dixon line as fast as this little car would take you."

"Wouldn't have missed it for the world," said her husband as he pulled her closer and kissed her soft cheek.

The Small and Shrinking World of Barney Blaine
2010

Barney came and went at will. At least this was his perception in the small world in which he lived. His thoughts were divided among a multitude of fears and anxieties based on accumulated indoctrinations from the slow-drip needle of life's lessons and hammered in right and wrong lessons (mostly from his mother's ceaseless lips) received early on with a quiet reverential awe and later (in his teen years) with all the resistance he could get away with. He had not yet learned to tune out, a technique he would perfect—the ability to shut his ears to her talk all the while smiling and nodding acceptance even approval of any critique—in his married life, his wife never knowing the better.

His incarceration or accommodation as it was sold to him had begun with a late night television infomercial claiming superiority for Tall Pines Retirement Community. All that he could want was wrapped in shiny paper and topped with the bow of contentment, glitter and peace, awe and calm, hyperactivity and sedation, all in one package. He bit. Now he was there secure and safe from the outside world at the same time isolated from his various pleasures, a state he had never anticipated or desired. *What good is a moat-less castle or a wall-less fort?* When did he begin to plot and plan his escape? Probably it was one Friday evening during the scheduled dinner—he was to appear at the door to the cafeteria no earlier than 5:45 and no later than 6:05, this was written law for the third shift diners—when Marie Whistler perhaps the most gregarious of the residents asked him to accompany her to the Saturday dance in the rooftop ballroom. It was clear to him her invitation was not spontaneous but a carefully contrived plot to get him. *Look at her over-made face. She has one long jet-black eyebrow for God's sake. Powder is falling from her ancient face and she is wearing cocktail party clothes. Jewels and gold are weighing her down. She smells of Listerine and some oversweet perfume. She is stalking no question about it.* Escape became not a possible move but an imperative. Thus began long sleepless nights of plans and stratagems (written down there would be material for a long novel) thought out and refigured many times owing the fact that escape involved eluding not only the local authorities but also his children, yes, even his accountant, lawyer, and minister.

Barney and Elizabeth were married in August, a month too hot for closeness except, of course, in the case of resolute passion. He had accumulated a small nest egg, laying aside the change from his pocket each evening when he removed his key and knife and rabbit's foot and the lint of the day. He thought her beautiful, too pretty for him, but deep inside—if he would have allowed himself the slightest glimpse—he would have seen himself standing high above her looking down on a lesser intellect and breathing deep the over-oxygenated air of the superincumbent. Elizabeth in her own mind, he had surmised, while uninformed and small-brained possessed a ton of confidence. He often thought of her brain as filled with red cells of certainty shoving the blue cells of knowledge and yes even common sense into stifled corners and narrow cul-de-sacs. But they apparently loved their differences in the beginning and were saturated with a passion that was brought on by those differences and were so wrapped up in satisfying the urges of youth and biological needs that many months passed before they discovered they had in reality no real love for each other. She was this first. He knew this because she grew cold to his touch and distant in her look. He realized the absence of love when he was denied her body and saw no need to pursue anything else she had to offer.

The move to Nebraska did not help. Barney brought with him Faulkner, Hemmingway, and Fitzgerald. Elizabeth left behind Harper, Mississippi—her father practically owned the town—and the Southern Baptist Church with its activities and rituals. He was content riding miles across flat lands to call on country doctors promoting the latest antibiotic or anti-hypertensive. She was stranded. Her discontent was demonstrated in a manner Barney thought of as passive aggressive. She was fighting for her life. She felt he had brought her to this cold place in her life and she isolated the problem as one would quarantine a contagion. He turned to infidelity.

But they stayed with each other, had three children together—her need for sperm, nothing more—raised them, educated them (both formally and in the ways of non-love), and pursued and achieved the identical life of so many of their neighbors and friends.

It was Barney who decided to commit himself to Tall Pines. His motivation while a little garbled in his mind was centered on his horror of needing, truly needing Elizabeth. If his health failed, as it was sure to do one day, maybe soon, he knew she would buckle down and do what was necessary to provide care for him. She would do much of the care herself, nursing and feeding him, keeping him alive. She would hate every minute of it and hate him too, even the more. Barney could not have that.

Now, he was incarcerated, unvisited by his wife (she would be too embarrassed by their separation) or children (who felt he was the villain in all this) and generally left to a new life (rebirth at age 74.) Life is always a comedy, he thought, unless it's your life.

Barney Blaine had always had a good memory. He still remembered the states and their capitals in alphabetical order, in fact, when waiting in line or for an appointment or when on hold for a phone call, he practiced recalling them. The rulers of England, France, Germany, and Russia were available to his recollection. The U.S. Presidents and their wives and even the Vice Presidents were part of his repertoire. This was all well and good, but with his lonely exile by Elizabeth came a deeper probe into his stored memory. He had read that the brain forgets certain events in order to make room for new data. But he had also read that the human brain was far under-utilized. Barney liked this concept better and set about trying to remember events from his childhood in detail. One night while he was still at home Barney was sitting in his lounger watching the local news. His face was still red from a confrontation with Elizabeth over a cup he had left on the side of the sink. It seemed to him the list of rules he was expected to follow for the privilege of living in his own house had grown considerably in the last week. How did he come to this? If he could go back maybe as far as high school and make better decisions his life would have to be better. But you can't go back. Well not really, but at least you have your memories. He thought of his senior prom and Eleanor Hendley. How deep could he delve into that one moment? What was she wearing? It was blue. The smell of her hair.

The music comes from a vividly lighted jukebox—The Platters' "My Prayer"—the band is taking a break. Eleanor pulls him closer. There is perfume in her hair. Her face is warm against his face. Her hands are cold. She moves ever so slightly, just enough to touch the corner of her lips to the corner of his lips. Surely he would be able to kiss her goodnight. He feels his heart beating. Or is it hers?

"Barney, what's the matter with you? Are you in a trance or something? I just don't know about you." Elizabeth stood over him.

"Just thinking about something."

"If you would put that much concentration into your work we'd be millionaires. Am I not right?"

"Yeah, you're right."

His game became an obsession and he welcomed his lonely study where he could swim around in his past with more and more accuracy of detail. He theorized that if he could just concentrate completely without interruption it would parallel time travel—he could actually return to those moments and only those moments that he chose.

It is the coldest of nights. The light from her windows lures him in, but he has already decided. On the table there is pot roast with potatoes, onions, and carrots. The wine is red and far too sweet. Her eyes say yes. He tries not to think of Elizabeth.

One would assume reliving the past an ideal situation. And this was true at first (his expectations were low.) But as Barney dug deeper and deeper in those moments, he began to lose his way back. Barney's assessment of his progress: two things were holding him back. First, experience and wisdom seemed to always get in the way. A foolish act of youth is hard to accept. If one is true to the project it has to be entered into with the understanding that foolishness must be left standing. Corrections in direction or purpose, made now, muddle the scene. The trip must be, from beginning to end, solely within the confines of memory. All adjustments must be squashed. And a more difficult dilemma: holding on to a single event. Related circumstances were always trying to enter the stage. Characters changed, no matter how implausible. Eleanor became Elizabeth became the others. Mississippi became Nebraska.

This frustrated Barney and literally made his head spin—not to mention a mild nausea that came upon him.

The lights of Hammond, Louisiana shine on the left. Only the light from an occasional house or the security light of a closed business is visible on the right. The familiar smell of the passenger train—burning tobacco and a mixture of oils, creams, and lotions leaking from the clothes and bodies of the riders—is at once pleasing and irritating. Billy Randall keeps nodding off. Billy, wake up. Let's smoke the rest of these cigarettes before we get home. The restroom is clear. Billy jumps up at the thought of pursuing the evil act. The pack of Lucky Strikes has only four remaining. They light one with the other to finish and deodorize before arriving home. Mid-smoke the conductor bangs on the door. What are you boys up to? No smoking or I'll tell your daddies. Was he serious or was he making fun of them? Quick puffing the remaining cigarette they laugh and relive the highlights of their trip to New Orleans. A free ride on the Illinois Central—a perk provided by their fathers' employment on the I.C.—made the excursion possible. Alan Ladd in "Shane." Best western ever made said Billy. That Jack Wilson was the meanest bastard that God ever let live. You're the meanest bastard that God ever let live said Elizabeth. She has the look of murder in her eyes.

"Damn, damn, damn," he said aloud. "Now I have to start over again. Maybe I can take up where I left off. No. That didn't work last time."

"What's the matter, honey," said Mrs. Morgan.

Barney looked at her white hair and her white uniform in disbelief.

"Who are you?"

"Mr. Blaine, you know who I am. I'm here with you every day except Wednesdays when I have to take mother to her doctor's appointment. Let's get you ready for Miss Elizabeth's visit."

"Elizabeth's coming here?"

"You silly boy. You know she comes almost every day. Never known a more devoted wife."

An early evening April breeze blows over Harper, Mississippi carrying away the steam from an afternoon shower. Honeysuckle fills the air. Elizabeth comes down with one knock on the door. She hugs him. I'll ask tonight. His eyes cannot wait. They ask her then and there. But he knows he will have to say it later, maybe in the porch swing. He can hardly make it through the movie. They hold hands and he asks her again with his touch. The swing squeaks out a song. His arm is around her. He asks her again with a kiss. She responds with a shiver. Will you? Yes. Yes.

That Moment

Joseph Campbell wrote:
(may I paraphrase)
The way to find happiness
is to keep your mind on those
moments when you felt most happy.
Not excited, not just thrilled.
But deeply happy.

Today, I felt alone.
My family moved around in their own world.
There seemed to be no room for me.
Not to worry, it's just today, I told myself.

But I tried it anyway, this Campbell thing.
I closed my eyes and looked way back.
And I saw her sitting on the gray front steps.
Her and both children,
the little girl still content by her side,
not yet a hint of approaching independence,
the son pushing a miniature red car,
back and forth across the bottom step,
beginning his own adventures.

I knew they were waiting for me.
And I felt they were saying thank you.
Thank you for going to work today.
Thank you for being a part of our lives

Edwards Brothers Malloy
Thorofare, NJ USA
April 15, 2014